ESPECIALLY FOR GIRLS™
presents

THAT SPECIAL SOMEONE

Gail Jarrow

The Berkley Publishing Group

That Special Someone

1

My friend Bethany has a way of getting me to do things I don't want to do. I'm not sure how she manages it, but she can convince me to forget my misgivings and go along with her schemes. Usually I end up regretting it.

Today, for example, I'd spent the whole morning raking leaves off Gram's lawn and carting them down to her compost pile behind the garage. For as long as I can remember, raking had been my older brother Ralph's job. Now that he is a big-shot optometrist with his own office, which unfortunately is open all day Saturday, it's my responsibility.

By the time Bethany rode up on her ten-speed wearing her brand-new jeans and tightest sweater, my arms felt as though I'd just rowed across the Atlantic in a dinghy.

"Go get cleaned up and we'll bike to the mall," she said, smoothing her long black hair.

"Not me. I'm exhausted."

"Raking doesn't make your legs tired. Anyway, we need to buy that folder for history class. Let's go."

I should have realized that Bethany was up to something. She couldn't care less about history class. But I cared — and she knew it. Within 15 minutes, I was following Bethany out Church Street on my rusty three-speed.

"Why are you going that way?" I asked as she turned off onto Creek Road. "It takes twice as long and the hill is a killer."

"The scenery's nice."

That's when I noticed that scheming look in her eyes. "Try again, Beth."

She slowly glided to a halt. "Well, I thought since you wanted to go to the mall. . ."

"*I* wanted to go?"

"Since we were going, we might as well go this way."

"This wouldn't have anything to do with a certain tall, handsome basketball player who just happens to live on Creek Road, would it?"

Bethany coyly raised her left eyebrow. "Maybe."

I made a face at her. "You spend half your waking hours—correction, two-thirds—chasing guys. It's ridiculous."

"At least *I* catch a few," she sniffed as she hopped back on her bike. "We can ride by his house and maybe he'll be outside and see me. Then I can say hello to him."

"Seems like a lot of trouble just to say hello to someone. Can't you do that in school?"

"Oh, Jeffi, you have absolutely no sense about these things! If Frank sees me, he'll have to say something. Then I'll say something. And before you know it . . ." She snapped her fingers.

"What?"

She rolled her eyes. "You know how these conversations go!"

Actually, I had no idea how *those* conversations went. I could talk for hours with the guys in the band about the next concert. And I felt comfortable speaking with any boy in the entire sophomore class about dissecting frogs. But when it came to romantic conversations, I had about as much experience as an artichoke.

"Frank Keeley is, beyond a doubt, the neatest guy I've ever had as my Special Someone," Bethany said as we crossed the stone bridge. "By the way, who's your Special Someone this year, Jeffi?"

"Uh, I haven't thought about it yet." I pedaled faster and pulled in front of her.

"Hey, wait up!" she called after me. "We've been in school almost a month already. What do you mean you haven't picked a Special Someone. You have to. It's tradition."

Bethany had this crazy idea that a girl should be in love at all times. She would pick a boy and then devise a scheme for getting him to date her. If for some reason he didn't work out, she'd choose someone else. Last year, she went through ten Special Someones before winter vacation.

I, on the other hand, never had a single one. It seemed unnatural, and not very special, to plan ahead of time whom I was going to fall in love with. I hoped someday a boy would come along whom I really cared about, not a guy I'd get tired of in a few weeks or one who'd get tired of me.

The brisk October wind whipped my face as the road cut between two mowed hayfields. Bethany was right behind me. I knew she wasn't ready to drop the discussion yet.

"What about Matt Perkins?" she said, catching up to me. "He'd be a perfect Special Someone for you."

"I've known him since kindergarten. How can I get romantic about someone I knew when he sucked his thumb?"

Bethany braked suddenly. "Shush. There's Frank's house now!"

I couldn't help giggling. "Isn't this a little obvious, stopping right in front of his house?"

"I know what I'm doing." Bethany hopped off her seat and stooped down by the front wheel.

"What's wrong with your tire?" I bent over to look.

"Nothing. I'm pretending it's flat," she whispered.

"Oh, gee! The helpless female routine. I can't stand this. I'll meet you at the mall." I pushed off and headed up the Creek Road Hill, glad to be away from the scene of one of Bethany's more absurd performances.

Before long, I was breathing hard and my calf muscles ached. As I reached the top, I heard Bethany approaching from behind.

"Wait . . . for . . . me," she puffed. I was glad she was out of breath too. Served her right.

"Didn't your damsel-in-distress act work?" I said as we coasted down the other side toward the mall.

"He must not have been home," she muttered.

"Or else he was watching from inside and getting the laugh of his life."

"All right. Go ahead and make fun of me," Bethany said as we rode into the mall parking lot. "I'll get Frank, just you wait and see."

She probably would.

As I leaned my bike against a pole near the mall entrance, I heard someone call my name. "There's Pete Symons." Snapping my lock, I hurried toward the door.

"Come on, we've got better things to do," mumbled Bethany.

"Just a sec."

Pete was perched on the concrete wall next to the glass doors. Tall and skinny with legs that looked like stilts, Pete reminded me of a scarecrow with curly red hair. We'd been friends since second grade when he'd helped me build a tree house. I couldn't remember ever having seen him without a happy expression.

"Peter," I called to him, "has it slipped your mind that we had a bet about how many times the percussion section would lose the rhythm during Wednesday's band practice?"

"I didn't forget, Jeffi. Honest." He smiled broadly.

"Then when am I going to get my ice-cream sandwich?"

"Monday. One every day next week, I promise." He held up three fingers.

"I bet you aren't even a boy scout."

"Wanna bet on that, too?"

"Nope. I'll quit while I'm ahead." I laughed. Out of the corner of my eye, I saw Bethany glaring at me. "Well, we have to get going. Until lunch on Monday."

"At your mercy." Peter bowed. "Have fun shopping. You too, Bethany."

"Thanks, I'm sure we will," Bethany answered sourly.

When we were inside the mall, I turned to her. "You could have been more pleasant. Pete's one of the nicest guys around."

"Oh, Jeffi, you're impossible," she said impatiently.

"What's wrong with that?"

"What's wrong is that nobody will ever see you as dating material if you spend your time making silly bets about drums with guys like Pete. If you don't change one of these days, you'll never . . ."

"Never what?"

"Forget it. You'd better get with it, that's all."

"Oh, I see. I should dump a good friend like Pete and start chasing after every unattached male in sight." *The way you do*, I thought to myself.

"You have to branch out. This is a crucial year. You'd better make it count."

The way her hands were placed on her hips and the scolding tone of her voice reminded me of Mom. Sometimes I got the feeling that Bethany considered it her mission to educate me in the areas Mom had neglected. This was Bethany's favorite record: "How to Make Jeffi Popular." The next line would be "You may be a straight-A student and a musical whiz, but you've earned a big fat F in romance."

". . . a big fat F, Jennifer Anders. Do you hear me? An F!"

"I heard you."

"You make no effort at all."

"I have lots of friends."

". . . and I'm talking about *boy*friends, not friends who happen to be male. There is a difference, in case you haven't noticed."

"I noticed."

"You've got to concentrate on your social life, and for heaven's sake, graduate from those computer-brain types."

I thought back to last year. The closest I'd come to a date was a junior who wanted to take me to see his exhibit on desalination at the county science fair. Luckily, Gram had planned a family reunion and I had a good excuse. What an awful memory that would have been! My first date—to a science fair with a chemistry freak.

Bethany wasn't telling me anything I didn't know already. "I can't help it if none of the decent guys at Daniel Boone notices me."

"Yes, you can!" She wagged her finger at me. "You're attractive— and I'm very critical of appearance, so believe me, it's true. You have to be more aggressive. Let the guys know you're interested in them. Flirt a little. They expect it."

Bethany said it with such authority I knew it must be true. Some girls were experts at flirting. They could make every calculated move seem sincere and natural. Whenever I tried to flirt, I felt like an actress who said her lines so unconvincingly that the audience got up and left the theater. The entire process of getting guys to take notice seemed like a game—one I was losing.

"I can't act like that, Beth."

"Of course you can. It's part of the female instinct. You have to stop fighting it." She ran her long, tapered red fingernails through her hair.

"You don't know what you're talking about."

"Oh, really? Well, let Bethany give you an expert demonstration." She surveyed the center atrium of the mall. "See that guy over there?"

I followed her gaze to a tall blond leaning against the gazebo on the opposite side of the fountain from us. He was licking an ice-cream cone and watching the water in the fountain spurt up and down.

"You can't go up to a total stranger and . . ." I grabbed her arm.

"Sure I can."

"Well, I'm not going with you."

"Stop being so archaic." She pulled away and headed toward the gazebo.

"I don't know you!" I called after her. I ducked behind a huge planter full of artificial philodendrons. I didn't want that boy, whoever he was, to think I was part of this stupid game.

Peeking through the fake foliage, I watched Bethany walk up to the stranger and start talking as if she'd known him for years. And to my surprise, he smiled at her and spoke back. How did she do it?

A few minutes later, she came around the corner of my planter. "See how easy it is?" she said smugly. "He's almost 16. His family's in the process of moving here from Washington, D.C., and next week he'll be enrolling at Daniel Boone. What do you think?"

"You learned all that in two minutes?" I stared at her in amazement.

"Takes skill. Besides, I know how to handle athletic types."

I looked toward the gazebo. The boy was taking the final bite from his sugar cone. Even from a distance, I could tell he was good-looking. "What's his name?"

"I forgot to ask," said Bethany sheepishly. "But so what? We can find out when he shows up at school."

"How can you do such things?" I shook my head.

She patted my shoulder and smiled. "That's how the game is played, my friend."

2

When the alarm rattled me out of a dream, I reached over and shut it off. Then, just like every weekday morning, I pulled the pillow over my head and went back to sleep.

The alarm was for Mom's benefit. I always set it for 7:00, exactly when she was combing her hair in the next room. I'd followed the same routine for the last six years, ever since she had bought the alarm clock and said it was my responsibility to pack lunch, make breakfast, and get myself off to school. For the past six years, Mom had driven away to her job as a medical secretary certain that I was out of bed and getting dressed. And for as many years, I had been rolling over and going back to sleep until Gram woke me at 7:45.

On schedule, Gram hit the radiator pipe in the kitchen with a tablespoon, sending her signal up to me. I rubbed my eyes open and realized it was Monday again. I smelled the aroma of French toast and heard Gram close the refrigerator door below. My growling stomach propelled me into action.

I had to move faster than I did six years ago. Now I had to insert the contact lenses I had started wearing the past summer. And I took longer with my hair since it was shoulder length instead of that ear-lobe cut I'd had until a year ago. Even so, I managed to make it out of the house by 8:15. Sara, who walked to school with me each morning, said it was amazing. I considered it efficient. Of course, it couldn't be done without Gram's help.

A blanket of frost covered the back lawn. Soon I'd have to put away all those summer dresses that made me feel like a graceful butterfly and bring out the bulky sweaters that made me look like a polar bear. Groaning, I reached for my green cords and beige turtleneck.

At least my light brown hair looked presentable this morning. It always shone right after I washed it. I brushed it once more and stepped back to check the total "me" in the mirror. Staring at my reflection, I recalled how everyone said I looked like my father. Sometimes I wished I could remember his face, but he had died when I was four and my memory didn't go back that far. Right after his death, Ralph, Mom, and I came to live in Gram's house.

Clang, bang. Gram's signal again. I grabbed my books and hurried downstairs.

"You look chipper this morning, Jennifer." Gram smiled as I pushed open the swinging door into the kitchen. "Your breakfast is on the table."

"Grapefruit, ugh. Gram, you know I hate grapefruit."

"Keeps the system operating. Sprinkle some sugar on it." Gram blotted the bacon between two paper towels and placed it on my dish.

I reached for the sugar bowl. "Where's Ralph?"

"He had to drive to Philadelphia early this morning to pick up a shipment of frames."

The day was starting well. For a change, I wouldn't have to listen to Ralph's complaints and criticisms. "What's for lunch?"

"Meat-loaf sandwich." She placed the bag lunch on the table. "What's your schedule this afternoon? I have a meeting until 4:30."

"Band practice. I'll be home by five." I dribbled molasses over the French toast. "What meeting?"

"Oh, that silly Golden Age group. Frumpy old people. I don't know why I bother going. Something to do, I guess."

"Ha! I bet it's because of all those handsome, white-haired gentlemen."

"Now don't you say a word to your mother or brother, Miss Smarty-pants! They think I'm too old for that sort of thing." She playfully threw her towel at me. I caught it before it hit my head.

There was a knock at the back door. "Oh, no, Sara already. Let her in, Gram. I'll get my clarinet and books."

When I returned to the kitchen, Sara was munching a piece of bacon. We'd been friends since her family moved down the street at the beginning of sixth grade. Although Sara was on the chubby side, she had a cute face with short blonde hair that accented her blue eyes. The best thing she had going for her was her outgoing personality. Everybody liked Sara and it was easy to see why. She could make even the shyest person feel comfortable.

"Hey, your yard looks great," she said as we walked across the grass to the sidewalk. "No more leaves, eh?"

"Not a single one. And I've got the blisters to prove it."

"Old Man Harvey ought to do something about his place. He always seems to have twice as many leaves as anyone else on the block and is the last to rake."

I chuckled. A few years ago, Gram had the hedges around the yard removed. The first time there was a big wind, our leaves blew across the street into Old Man Harvey's yard. He stood on our porch for an hour huffing and cussing, but Gram didn't even come to the door. Every year, the same thing happened.

"Did you do your algebra yet?" Sara asked.

"Last night." Once Ralph suggested I do my weekend homework on Friday. After that, I made a point of doing it only on Sundays.

"I'm going to try to get mine done in study hall. I was in charge of my little brothers all weekend since Mom and Dad had to work. I couldn't get to it."

"Don't worry, it's easy."

"You should have seen what happened on Friday," she said as we crossed Church Street. "Diana confronted Ron about Clarissa and it looks like Jonathan is going to divorce his wife and marry that nurse."

"No kidding," I said sarcastically. Sara didn't notice. She continued to give me the complete soap-opera rundown as she did every morning.

"I have to stay after school to make up an English test today. Could you watch for me?"

"Can't. Have band." Sara always tried to get me to watch. I didn't want to get hooked too.

"Maybe your Gram would. I should have asked her."

"She has a meeting. You won't miss that much in one day."

"Oh, yes, I will. So much can happen! But I suppose I can ask Cheryl Jones. She never misses." Sara looked at her watch. "Hey, we'd better hurry or we'll be late. Are you walking slowly today or is it my imagination?"

"My legs still hurt from riding up the Creek Road Hill."

"What were you doing on Creek Road?"

"Ask Bethany."

"Frank Keeley, right? Leave it to Beth to figure some way to track him down. What did she try this time?"

"Don't ask," I moaned. "How about quizzing me on the Spanish vocabulary? I always clutch on Señora's tests."

"Come off it, Jeffi. You've never gotten anything lower than a 90 in your life. I bet you could recite those words in your sleep."

I shook my head. "Spanish is my hardest subject. I've worked like crazy to get my A in there and I don't want to blow it on this test. Please?"

"Well, OK," Sara replied as the light at Main Street turned green. We hurried across. "Do you want Spanish or English first?"

"English." If my mind hadn't been so wrapped up in Spanish translations, I would have handled what happened next more calmly. But it was and I didn't.

The gray Chevy Nova came out of nowhere and screeched to a halt along the curb next to us. The horn blasted twice and a masculine voice called out from inside the car, "Wanna ride, cuties?"

I took one look at the car with its dented fender, remembered Mom's "strange-car" lectures, and grabbed Sara's arm. "Let's get out of here!" I started running.

I'd only gone a few yards when Sara's laughter made me turn around. "What's wrong with you? It's only my cousin Sam and his girl friend. Come back here and get in. We're late anyway."

What I needed at that moment was a magic genie to save me from complete embarrassment. He could conjure up a Doberman to snap at my heels so I'd have an excuse for running away. Or, better yet, he could give me a new face so no one would recognize me. As I crawled into the back seat next to Sara, I knew all I could do was to sink down in the seat and hope Sam and his girl friend would forget I was there.

"Sam, Gloria, do you know Jeffi Anders?" Sara said cheerfully. Just what I needed.

"I've seen her passing through Senior Hall a few times," Sam replied.

Gloria turned around and smiled.

I smiled back and sunk even lower. Then for the first time, I realized someone else was in the back seat on the other side of Sara. If only my genie would help me vanish into thin air.

There he sat, looking as if he belonged on a movie screen. Mike Hauser, Daniel Boone Senior High's football hero. No one was quite like Mike. He was built like a junior Mr. Universe and taller than most of the other guys. His jet-black hair was thick and wavy and looked perfectly groomed even on windy days. He had the darkest eyes I'd ever seen and the longest lashes possible without the aid of mascara.

Since the first day of high school last year, when the rest of us humbly entered the halls of Daniel Boone, Mike had acted as if the place belonged to him. Nobody intimidated him—not teachers, not principals, not upperclassmen. Mike Hauser was at the center of everything exciting that happened.

Sara leaned over the front seat. She didn't seem the least bit unnerved by Mike's presence only inches away. "How come you're over on this side of town, Sam?"

"I had to take Dad to work. His car wouldn't start. That's a switch, isn't it?" replied Sam. "Mike missed his bus so I gave him a lift too. Must be my day for good deeds."

"Are you psyched for the Boyerville game Friday night?" Sara said, turning to Mike.

"Sure." He cracked his knuckles. "And you'd better be there cheering." He winked at me.

Grinning awkwardly, I nodded. If only I could think of a witty reply.

Three blocks later, we pulled up in front of the sprawling, brick high school. "Hope you don't mind if I drop you fledglings off here before Gloria and I head over to Senior Wing," said Sam.

"Thanks for the ride," I said, opening the door. Sara and Mike slid out behind me.

The chilly morning had chased most kids from their regular hangouts on the wide lawn into the warmth of the lobby. At that moment, the front lawn never seemed so empty nor the lobby door so far away. I couldn't remember ever having felt this tongue-tied and nervous.

We were halfway up the sidewalk when Sara stopped. "Darn! I think I dropped my pen when I got out of the car. I'd better go back and look for it. You two go ahead. I'll catch up."

Suddenly, there I was—alone with Mike Hauser, walking shoulder to shoulder into the building. Should I say something or let him initiate a conversation? I'd already made a fool of myself once this morning. I didn't want to do it again. My stomach felt as knotted as a macramé belt.

"I've been meaning to tell you something, Jeffi." Mike smiled as he opened the lobby door for me. His teeth were ultra-white and straight as piano keys. "You've been looking real good this year."

Was I dreaming? Did he say what I thought he said? I didn't even think he knew my name. I tried to force out a "thank you," but it wouldn't come. What would Bethany say at a moment like this?

I stood frozen in the doorway, looking at Mike and trying to get my lips to move. The next thing I knew Sara was nudging me inside. I was in such a daze that I hadn't heard her come up behind me.

"I think she looks better too. It's her longer hair and the contact lenses, don't you think? Those glasses she used to wear made her look too studious."

"Yeah, maybe that's it." Mike smiled at me again. "Well, see you around, Jeffi."

I watched him cross the lobby toward his clique standing near the auditorium door. Most of the football players were there. So were Patricia O'Reilly and Dyan Warren, two sophomores who always positioned themselves near the most popular guys.

My stomach was still turning flip-flops when Bethany rushed down the hall, her eyes wide with excitement. "What's going on?" She lowered her voice to almost a whisper. "You came to school with Mike Hauser!"

"Sam gave us a ride," Sara replied. "And listen to this part. Mike told Jeffi she was looking 'real good' this year." She imitated Mike's deep voice and batted her eyelashes at me.

I shrugged and headed toward my locker. But Bethany wasn't about to let me off the hook that easily. She caught my arm. "We can't talk here with all these ears around." She threw a sideward glance at a few girls standing nearby. None of them was paying any attention. "Let's go to the girls' room on the band hall. No one will be there now."

They each grabbed an arm and practically pulled me down the hall.

"This is crazy," I protested as Sara closed the bathroom door.

"What did you say after he told you that?"

"She didn't say anything," Sara answered before I could open my mouth. "Can you believe it? The neatest guy in school makes a comment like that and Jeffi doesn't say a word."

Bethany looked shocked.

"I couldn't think of anything intelligent to say." I rested my clarinet case and knapsack on the ledge under the mirror and took out my comb. I wished they would stop making such a fuss.

Bethany put her hands on her hips, her maternal pose. "*You* couldn't think of anything intelligent? That's a first."

"I don't know what came over me. I just clammed up."

The two girls exchanged looks. "Could this be Jeffi's first crush?" teased Sara, putting her arm around my shoulders.

I jammed the comb back into the knapsack. "I've had crushes before."

"And we're going to see that you do something about it this time," Bethany said.

"All he did was say a few words to me. He didn't even mean them, I'm sure." I picked up my stuff. "I'm going to homeroom."

I pushed open the bathroom door and hurried down the hall. I could imagine what they were thinking. How inexperienced I was, a dunce with guys. How I'd blown my big chance with Mr. Wonderful. But what did they expect? I wasn't used to handsome football players paying me compliments. I threw my jacket into the locker and slammed the door. The metal clang echoed through the hall.

Mr. Mowrer came out of homeroom. "Better hurry before the bell rings, Jennifer."

"Yes, sir." I brushed by him and slid into my seat in the first row. The room buzzed with conversation and laughter.

"What's with you this morning?" Mary Anderson whispered as I leaned back in my chair. "You look as if you don't know whether you're coming or going."

"I don't," I sighed as the 9:00 bell announced the beginning of a new day.

I went through the whole day in a fog. In Spanish class, Señora Martinez caught me daydreaming and stood over my desk for two minutes ranting and raving in Spanish. Fortunately I couldn't understand anything she said. In algebra fourth period, Mr. Trimble sent me to the board to do a homework problem and I did the wrong one without even realizing it. I even forgot to collect my ice-cream sandwich from Pete at lunch. It was a relief when band practice ended and I could finally go home where no one would notice how unhinged I was.

There was no doubt about it. The episode with Mike Hauser had thrown me off balance. I still felt quivery when I thought about it. But I knew I had to be logical. Mike was one of the most popular guys in school and I was . . . well, I simply was not in his league. His comment was just small talk. He forgot he'd said it two minutes after the words left his mouth. If Bethany and Sara hadn't blown the whole thing out of proportion, I wouldn't have given it another thought. Conclusion: it made no sense to waste another day thinking about Mike Hauser.

When I walked in the front door, Gram was standing in the hall holding out the phone to me. "For you, Jennifer. You're lucky I heard you coming up the porch steps or I would have hung up."

I put my knapsack on the hall chair and took the phone.

"It's a boy," she whispered.

A boy? Calling me? I tried to stop myself, honest I did. But my hands started getting clammy and I felt the fog coming over me again. Maybe Bethany and Sara were right about Mike after all.

"Jeffi?" The voice was familiar.

"Yes."

"I didn't want you to think I forgot . . ."

Familiar, but not Mike's.

". . . but you ran out of band so fast, I didn't get a chance to talk to you."

The fog lifted. "It's OK about the ice cream, Pete. I forgot all about it myself."

"Tomorrow, I promise."

"Yeah, sure. That'll be fine."

"Are you all right, Jeffi? You sound depressed or something."

"No, Peter. All's well," I said in a more cheerful voice. "Don't forget or I shall seek revenge."

"I shall not. Farewell for now."

When I entered the kitchen, Ralph and Mom were already at the table and Gram was taking rolls from the oven.

"About time you got home," Ralph said as I washed my hands in the sink. "I'm starving."

"It wouldn't hurt you to miss a meal once in awhile." I sat down across from him.

Ralph scowled. He had a lousy sense of humor.

"You *were* rather late, Jennifer." Mom passed the peas to me.

"I had band. I helped clean up afterward." I knew she'd believe that. Actually I couldn't figure out why it had taken me so long to walk home. Must have been the fog.

"Well, I wish you'd be more considerate," Ralph said. "I have a date tonight and I don't want to be late."

I felt like saying "Who would want to date you?", but I didn't. He might say the same thing to me.

"And what about Gram's dinner?" he continued. "She shouldn't have to keep it warm because of you."

There's nothing worse than a 27-year-old brother who thinks he can talk to you like a father. "Look, Ralph, I've had to bend over backwards for you plenty of times. Just cut it out."

"Could we stop this and have a peaceful meal, please?" Mom looked at Ralph and me. Mostly at me, as usual.

"Amen," Gram added as she plopped mashed potatoes on her dish.

Mom got her wish. We had another peaceful, boring meal. For most of dinner, Mom explained to Ralph how he could do his billing more efficiently if he followed the routine they used in her office. Then Gram talked about the speaker at her Golden Age meeting. Finally, by dessert, after everyone had a say, I was included in the conversation.

"How was your day, Jennifer?" asked Mom as she took a bite of her carrot cake. It bothered me when she talked with her mouth full since she jumped on me for doing it.

"Ms. Morgan made me a committee chairman for our history presentations."

"What's your topic, dear?" Gram asked.

"The Civil War, but we haven't decided anything specific yet. I know we'll have the best presentation, even if I do have a couple of hack-offs to work with. I'll think up a terrific skit that Ms. Morgan will love."

Ralph stared at me over his coffee cup. "What makes you think someone else on your committee won't have a better idea?"

"I just know." I glared at him. Why couldn't he let up on the negative comments occasionally? I'd teach him a lesson tonight.

"Good dinner, Mother," said Mom as she poured her second cup of coffee. That was my cue to clear the table.

Gram smiled as I removed her plate and took it to the counter. "Next week at Golden Age that nice Mr. Orb from the insurance company is showing slides of his trip to the Northwest."

"That should be very interesting." Mom pushed her plate toward me.

"Ralph, do you remember the capital of Washington State?" I said as I cleared his place. "I can't recall."

"Tacoma," he replied without hesitating. He's always so sure of himself.

"I thought it was Seattle." Mom took the bait, too.

"How sure are you, Ralph?"

"Positive. I know it's not Seattle."

"Want to place a bet?" Mom said smiling. It was working perfectly. I'd hooked them both.

"Sure. How about a dollar?"

"OK. Go get the atlas, Jennifer."

"Can I bet too?" I asked.

"I thought you didn't know the capital." Ralph looked at me as if he were starting to get the idea.

"Just a guess?"

"All right, what do you guess?" Mom said.

"Olympia."

"Is that a city in Washington? Never heard of it," Gram laughed.

"I'll get the atlas." It had worked again.

After I had collected their money, Ralph disappeared upstairs. He said he had to get ready for his date, but I knew it was because he hated losing, especially to me.

Mom, Gram, and I went into the living room to watch the news.

Gram always fell asleep on the couch the minute Dan Rather came on the screen. She was lucky she didn't have a current-events quiz every Friday.

"How did you know Olympia?" Mom asked during a commercial.

"I have tricks to remember all the capitals. For instance, when I think of Washington State, I think of Mt. Saint Helens volcano. That reminds me of Helen of Troy, which reminds me of the Greeks. And that reminds me of the Olympics."

"Not exactly direct, but it obviously works. Your memory amazes me."

I wondered if Mom knew her words meant more to me than the two dollars. Probably not.

After the news, I went upstairs. Tonight, for a change, I would have some privacy for Bethany's call. Usually I had to whisper when I wanted to say anything important. If only I had my own phone as she did. By the time the phone rang, Mom was at her library board meeting and Ralph had left for his date. Gram, who snapped awake as soon as Dan Rather signed off, was watching a "M.A.S.H." rerun. I don't think she even heard the ring.

"Jeffi, the best thing happened!" Bethany started almost before I had the phone to my ear. "Frank stopped by my locker after school. He was waiting there when I got out of P.E."

"That's super, Beth. I guess he likes you."

"You bet he does. He even asked me if I'm going to the dance Saturday."

"Did he ask you to go with him?"

"*Really*, you can't expect that already. But this is the first step." I imagined her sitting in her bedroom, drawing hearts with Frank's name inside all over her phone book. "And me with my hair still wet from the shower Miss H. made us take."

"It would have been worse if you hadn't had a shower."

"He walked me out to the flagpole and we waited for his bus together. I felt so special being with him. As if I were his girl."

I wondered what that special feeling was like.

"Now we'll work on you. You *have* to go to the dance. It's the first one this year and I know Mike will be there."

"Would you cut it out?"

"What *are* you going to do about him?"

"Nothing to look stupid, I'll tell you that!"

"Don't blow this. Make an effort, for a change. Let me help you. I can show you how it's done."

"I'll think about it."

"You'd better. Look, I have to call Sara and fill her in about Frank. Talk to you tomorrow."

I walked back the dark hall to my bedroom. The guffaws of the canned laugh track floated up the stairs from the living room. I shut my door and began writing down the major stories from the evening news in my current-events journal. But I couldn't keep my mind on interest rates and defense spending very long.

Bethany was right. I hadn't made much effort with guys. But why should I want to encourage the kind of guys who were interested in me? A dissertation on desalination isn't the sort of thing to make a girl's heart flutter. As for chasing the more popular guys—I never thought I had a chance, so why bother? Now Bethany was making me think I'd been wrong about that. I got up from my desk and stood in front of the full-length mirror on my closet door.

> Mirror, mirror, can you see,
> Will someone fall in love with me?

Maybe playing games was the only way to get guys to notice you. Bethany, Dyan, and Patricia did it and they had guys falling all over them. You can't argue with success. Maybe if I knew more of the rules, I could win too. One thing I knew: unless I wanted to be one of those girls who goes through high school without a single date, I had to take action.

"Well, Mike, I haven't decided about the dance yet, but if I go, I'd simply love to dance with you. That is, unless someone else asks me first.

"Oh, thank you, Mike. I'm glad you like my dress. Really? Blue is my favorite color too. We have a lot in common.

"That was a wonderful play you made in the game. You were absolutely terrific. I'm sure the team would never get a single touchdown if it weren't for you."

"Jennifer, are you still on the phone, dear?"

I opened my door and shouted downstairs, "No, Gram, I'm doing my homework."

"I thought I heard you talking just now."

"Must have been the radio."

I looked at myself in the mirror again. This was going to take lots of practice.

3

My skin tingled every time I thought about the dance, but I was careful not to let Bethany or Sara know. They were both so busy planning what to wear that neither would have noticed even if I hadn't been trying to hide it.

On Friday night, the band played the half-time show at the football game. Usually I spent the game watching people walk around the track next to the field or talking to other girls in band who were as disinterested in football as I was. But this time, I had my eyes glued on the field, stuck on Number 10, Mike Hauser. I wasn't sure if he were playing well or not. It didn't really matter. The thrill was watching him throw the ball or run across the field. I could almost feel the pain when he was tackled and hear his voice calling plays in the huddle. How I wished I had been one of the cheerleaders who rushed over to hug him when we won!

If I hadn't had my hands full baby-sitting for the Donnelly kids on Saturday afternoon, I would have been a nervous wreck before I even started dressing for the dance. Cleaning peanut butter off the kitchen floor and reading *Cat in the Hat* 25 times was enough to keep my mind off Mike—at least temporarily.

At dinner, I skipped dessert—it was only pudding anyway—and cleared the table before Mom's signal. I wanted to have plenty of time to get dressed. My clothes were already laid out on my bed;

I'd planned my outfit all week. Of course, whenever Sara or Bethany asked me, I said I wouldn't bother thinking about it until Saturday night.

I spent 15 or 20 minutes in the shower washing and rewashing my hair, but for once Gram didn't bang on the door to tell me I was wasting hot water. I used the strawberry-scented shampoo Mom won at the new drugstore's grand opening. After I fixed my hair with the styling brush, it fell in soft curls on my shoulders. I added a little make-up—not too much or Mom would send me back upstairs to scrub it off—and a few drops of perfume to my neck. Just in case Mike got close enough. Not bad, I thought, examining myself in the bathroom mirror.

> Mirror, mirror, tell me right,
> Will I dance with Mike tonight?

"Bethany and Sara just pulled up." Mom was looking out the front window as I came down the stairs. The excitement I had suppressed all week was about to break through. I hoped I could hold it in until I got out of the house.

"Whew! You smell like a cosmetics store," Ralph said as he and Gram entered the hallway from the living room. "What's so special about this dance? Has Jeffi finally noticed boys?" He laughed, but not in a particularly nice way, if you ask me.

"I think she looks beautiful." I could count on Gram to say something complimentary.

"Here's your coat," Mom said. "Don't keep them waiting."

"You be out on the curb at 11:00 sharp," Ralph ordered as he turned on the porch light.

"Yeah, yeah." I knew the only reason he agreed to pick us up was because Mom had plans for the evening and asked him to do it.

"I'm not kidding, Jeffi. I'm going hiking tomorrow and I have to get up early. So don't be late."

"*You'd* better be there."

Bethany's brother, Kevin, dropped us off at school. He said he didn't mind since he was going out anyway. Why couldn't I have a brother like that?

We'd only been in the dimly lighted gym for two minutes when Bethany announced she'd checked out every corner and that, indeed, all the right people were here. "There's Frank by the soda table. I don't want to stare. Does he see me?"

Sara and I both peered in his direction.

"Don't you stare either! It's too obvious," she whispered.

"Go over and say hello," I said. "After all, he sort of asked you to come, didn't he?"

"I can't do *that*, Jeffi! Tell her, Sara."

"Relax, Beth. You're acting like a nervous giraffe." Sara clicked her tongue.

I felt as though a herd of nervous giraffes were galloping (or whatever giraffes do) in my stomach, but I was determined not to show it. "Look at those ninth-graders bunched over by the windows. Did we do that last year?"

"Probably. Let's move away from the door so we don't look as scared as they do." Sara headed for a crowd of other sophomores. Bethany and I followed. It was a good thing the giraffes weren't bothering Sara or we might have spent the night in the doorway.

The Pep Club, which sponsored the dance, had decorated the gym using a fall sports theme. At one end stood a cardboard goal post wrapped in green-and-white streamers. The disc jockey and his turntable were located beneath it. Along the wall opposite the bleachers was a soccer cage. In front of it, the soda table was adorned with "Hornets can't be beat" and "Sting them" posters. The walls were covered with colorful murals of cross-country, field hockey, football, and soccer players. A large portion of the gym floor near the disc jockey was marked off for dancing. Strobe lights above the dance floor flashed with the beat of the music.

Gradually the gym filled up. The air was charged with excitement, maybe because of the football victory, or maybe because this was the first dance of the year.

At last, the moment I had anticipated arrived. Mike came in the door. He strode across the floor with such confidence that you'd think the dance was a party thrown in his honor. Laughter, back-slapping, and hugs from Patricia and Dyan greeted him as he approached the area around the D.J.'s table where his friends had staked out their territory. He was their leader.

Lead me. I'll follow.

It didn't take Mike long to grab a girl and start dancing. He looked as if he belonged in one of those advertisements for men's cologne. Blue cords a bit snug around his muscular thighs; a red-and-blue plaid shirt unbuttoned at the neck; dark hair just touching the collar. I bet he smelled good, too.

"Wanna dance?" Leon Bolonna stood ogling me.

"OK," I said unenthusiastically. Just my luck. A slow dance.

Leon, who had been in my math class last year, was one of those kids who had never lost his baby fat. He kept manufacturing more. You couldn't see exactly how fat he was by looking at him because he wore bulky sweaters all the time. Dancing with him, I could tell, and it was disgusting. When he put his arms around me, I thought I was being smothered by a huge mohair sweater. After he finally released me and I escaped to Sara's side, my turtleneck was covered with tiny wool fuzzies.

"What happened to Bethany?" I asked Sara as I brushed off my shirt.

"Hook-shot Frank finally made his move." She nodded toward the dance floor where Bethany and Frank were occupied. Near them, I spotted the plaid shirt and blue cords with a new partner. At least he wasn't spending the whole evening with one girl.

"Try not to look as if you're dying to dance with him, Jeffi."

"What are you talking about?"

"Play it casual. He'll ask you, I know it. But don't look so lovesick."

Soon I was too busy dancing to keep my eye on Mike. It was better than sitting in the bleachers, otherwise known as Wallflower Row. On the other hand, the guys who asked me weren't my idea of perfect partners.

Paul Lambert danced like a marionette about to break its strings. The way he threw his arms around during a fast number made me wish I had on a combat helmet for protection. And there was Rob Samuels who slow-danced by rocking from one foot to the other. If the song had been a lullaby, I would have fallen asleep. Then came Brad Tompkins, who was a terrific dancer, and cute too. The problem was that he was two inches shorter than I. Fast dancing was fine, but it was awkward when the slow music started. I tried to shrink by bending my knees. It didn't work.

Just as Leon lumbered toward me again, Pete Symons appeared, his curly hair mussed, as usual. I wondered if he ever combed it. "You've saved me from a fate worse than death. I'm indebted to you."

"What?" he asked.

"Never mind."

"How about if I get you a soda? You look as if you could use it."

"Good idea." I wiped the perspiration off my forehead.

"My treat. Then we'll be even on the bet."

We battled our way through the crowd to the soccer cage. The outside door next to the soda table was open and a refreshing breeze greeted us.

"Pretty decent dance, isn't it?" asked Pete, gulping down his soda.

"I haven't missed your escapades with Mary Yardley, if that's what you mean."

"You haven't been sitting out the night either, good buddy." He crumpled his cup and threw it in the trash can. His eyes were fixed on the hallway entrance. Mary was returning to the gym, probably after a trip to the girls' room.

"Do you mind if I . . . uh . . ."

"Go ahead, Romeo," I laughed. "And thanks for the soda."

As I sipped the last of my drink, someone touched my arm. I swerved around. My heart stopped beating. It was Mike.

"Didn't mean to scare you, Jeffi. Having a good time?"

"Uh, yeah." An awkward pause. I tried to think of all those

things I'd planned to say in case this happened. My mind was blank.

"Good. I am too." He put a quarter on the table and picked up a cup. Crunching the ice with his perfect teeth, he gazed at the dance floor.

Silence. Excruciating silence.

I had to say something. He'd walk away in a second if I didn't. I swallowed the lump creeping up my throat. "You played a great game last night."

He turned as if he'd suddenly remembered I was there. "Hey, thanks! I was really pumped up. One of the best games we ever had, don't you think?"

I nodded.

"In the third quarter . . . wow! I was psyched to throw that one. I knew the minute the ball left my fingers that it was going to be perfect."

"It *was* a good throw," I said, acting as if I knew which play he was talking about.

"Of course, their defense was rotten. But even so, I think we played a top notch game."

"Especially you."

He shrugged. "Almost everyone played well. We were up for it. I know we'll slaughter Mount Penn next week. I can feel it in my arm." He grasped the bicep on his right arm and wiggled his long fingers.

We talked for at least ten minutes. Well . . . *he* talked, I listened. About the game. About how the coach said Mike was the best quarterback to come through Daniel Boone in years, even though he was still only a sophomore. About how he was lifting weights to build up his arms. The lump in my throat started to dissolve. It hadn't been hard to get Mike to notice me after all.

The disc jockey put on another slow dance. People around the soda table drifted to the dance floor until Mike and I stood there alone. I kept my eyes on him and pretended not to notice the exodus.

"I was so busy talking about the game," he said when the song was half-over. "I didn't hear them put on that McCartney record. How about it?" He motioned to the dance floor.

The next moment I was in his arms. As he held me against his chest, I closed my eyes. I was in a dream floating around the dance floor. I heard neither the music nor the murmur of voices around me. All I was aware of was Mike's breathing and the pressure of his hand on my back. He smelled even better than I'd imagined.

When the music stopped, he stepped back and smiled. A second later, he disappeared into the crowd around the disc jockey's table. I was left standing in the middle of the floor trying to figure out if I'd fantasized the whole thing.

"I saw it! I saw you and Mike!" Sara rushed over and grabbed my arm. "I knew it would happen."

It *had* happened.

"They always have a lady's choice, Jeffi. You have to ask him!"

The thought of asking Mike to dance gave me goose bumps. "I couldn't do that. Not in a million years."

"Why not? He asked you, didn't he? He must be attracted to you."

Sara made it seem logical. But then she had the nerve to ask any guy in the room to dance. What if the only reason he asked was because he felt foolish standing around while everyone else headed for the dance floor? "I don't think I should."

The disc jockey's voice came over the speakers and the gym quieted down. "The final slow dance of the evening will be a lady's choice. Come on, girls. This is your last chance."

"Go on." Sara pushed me in Mike's direction. "It's the perfect opportunity to show him you're interested."

Around the gym, girls approached guys and led them to the floor. It didn't look difficult. "But what if he says no?"

"Go ahead," Sara repeated.

I started across the gym. Flashing lights above the dance floor made the room whirl. My face was on fire. I tried to make my feet move faster, but they felt like lead. What if the song ended before I got to Mike?

I was only a few yards away. Mike glanced in my direction. Was he smiling? Did he want me to ask him? I had to go through with it now.

He looked away. I was sure he was smiling. Then I saw why. Dyan Warren swooped down and pulled him onto the dance floor. Holding hands and laughing, they brushed past me.

It was almost worse than if Mike had turned me down. I should have known better than to think I had a chance with someone like him.

4

The minute I woke up on Monday, I knew it was going to be one of those days that is miserable to live through and even worse to think about once it's over.

First, Mom was running late so she pounded on my door at 7:15. "Get up, Jennifer. You overslept."

"OK, OK," I called out to her as I put my pillow over my head. I'd been up late finishing an oral book report and I was exhausted. I had almost fallen back to sleep when Gram banged on the pipe. I glanced at the clock. 7:50! Gram's signal was five minutes late and my morning schedule was completely thrown off.

At breakfast, Ralph grumbled about how he was going to fire his secretary because she botched up his files. He claimed no one, including her, could find anything in them. Then Gram put Ralph's liverwurst sandwich in my lunch bag, which I discovered on the way to school when the odor began to nauseate me.

Since I was late, Sara went on without me. Maybe she would have cheered me up. As it was, the day grew more dismal with each step I took. It had rained the previous night and the air was damp and cold—the kind of weather when you can't get warm no matter how many clothes you put on. I had to watch where I walked because the pavements were a maze of puddles. Wet leaves made the air smell like a mildewed basement. Halfway to school, I realized

I should have brought an umbrella. It was sure to rain again, probably when I was walking home.

"Who's the morose moose?" Bethany said when I found her in the lobby.

"Cute, Beth."

"I want to hear all about you and Mike. You wouldn't tell me anything Saturday night."

"There's nothing to tell. Besides, I didn't have a chance to say a word in the car Saturday because you never stopped talking about Frank."

Bethany pushed her shining hair behind her ears. "All right, maybe I did get carried away. But now I want to hear about how he asked you to dance. Details, girl, details. I'm sure Sara left out the best parts. She always does."

I spotted Sara and Cheryl Jones leaning against the wall deep in conversation. About last week's soaps, no doubt. "I don't know if I'll ever go to another dance. My feet still hurt from dancing with Paul Lambert."

"Forget him. I want to hear about Mike Hauser."

"He's a neat guy, I guess."

"You guess? Oh, Jeffi, I can't stand it!"

The bell rang and we headed down the sophomore hall to our lockers. "Wait up, you two." Sara ran up behind us. "You won't believe what happened last Friday. Cheryl filled me in. Incredible! I can't miss it today. Did you tell Jeffi about the party yet?"

"What party?" I asked as Bethany stopped at her locker.

"I wasn't going to tell you until you were in a better mood." She fiddled with her combination.

"OK. I can wait. See you later." I knew that would get her.

"No, no, wait. Frank called me last night." Bethany was practically doing pirouettes. "He invited me to a Halloween party at Dyan Warren's house."

"What did your parents say?"

"Is that all you can ask, Jeffi? My Special Someone invites me to a party and you think of my parents."

It *was* the wrong thing to say. But it was the first thing I'd think of if my Special Someone asked me to a party at Dyan's. Then again, I'm not Bethany, and Mom isn't like Mr. and Mrs. Freedman, and I don't have a Special Someone. "Sorry, Beth. I'm excited for you. Really."

"Well, what *did* they say?" Sara asked.

For some reason, Bethany didn't find the question so offensive coming from Sara. "At first, they gave me a hard time. Then I reminded them how they let Kevin go to parties without interrogation. Mother gave in immediately. She brags to all her friends that she's raised Kevin and me the same. And Dad was a cinch to convince when I told him Frank played basketball. You know how he is about sports.

"Here comes Old Hook-shot himself," whispered Sara.

Bethany glanced at her reflection in the mirror on her locker door and smoothed her hair.

"She's on Cloud Nine," I said to Sara as we continued down the hall.

"More like Cloud Nine squared!" Sara laughed. "Hey, if you don't have anything better to do Halloween, how about coming over and helping me baby-sit for my brothers until my parents get off their shifts. Then we can go to the library and see the horror flick."

I stopped outside my homeroom. "Sounds like fun."

"If you get a better offer, let me know."

"You don't have to worry, believe me."

As I opened my locker door, I noticed Mike and his entourage parading down the hall. How could I have thought I had a chance with someone like him? When he had his pick of the "in" girls, why should he bother with me? Why did I make such a fool of myself over him? I grabbed my books and ran into homeroom before the group passed my locker.

My clarinet lesson was scheduled for second-period Spanish. It *was* going to be one of those days!

"Oh, Señorita Ahn-ders, no! No lección música! Not again,"

Señora Martinez cried, yanking at her hair. She was the most melodramatic person I'd ever met.

"I haven't missed your class for six weeks, Señora. I'll get the notes." I knew she'd let me go. But first I'd have to go through the whole routine.

She threw her arms in the air so vehemently that the blouse pulled out from her skirt. "What I endure!" She cradled her head in her hands. You'd think her entire family had been lost at sea. Most of the class was watching. It was an entertaining show.

"You may go if you can conjugate the verb *cantar*, to sing," she continued. She put her face right next to mine.

"Canto, cantas, canta, cantamos, cantan."

Pointing to the door with her yardstick, she screeched, "Adios!"

"Adios to you, too." I hurried out.

Norma Collins was putting her clarinet together when I entered the band room. Norma and I had been first clarinets all through junior high and last year when we joined the Freshman-Sophomore Band. We'd moved up in the section as the older kids went on to the Junior-Senior Band. Now I was first chair and Norma was second.

As I moistened my reed, I watched Norma warm up. It was amazing she could play as well as she did considering how long her fingernails were. Mr. Bonner wanted her to cut them so she could finger the keys faster. She wouldn't do it.

"Where's everyone?" I asked her.

"Aren't coming, I guess."

"How about Mr. Bonner?"

"Coffee, I think."

Norma may have long fingernails, but she's short on words. For four years, I sat next to her in band practice and she never once initiated a conversation.

"Have you practiced this piece much?" I pointed to the duet Mr. Bonner assigned last week.

She nodded.

"I thought it was hard."

Norma readjusted her reed.

"Norma? Earth calling Norma."

"Huh? Uh, yes, me, too."

Mr. Bonner came out of his office and pulled up a chair. "How are you both today?" He smiled as he looked over the duet on the music stand.

"Fine," I replied. Norma just nodded.

"Before we start, I want to tell you about a new system we're going to use this year."

I had a feeling I wasn't going to like this.

"Instead of my deciding who sits in the first chair or second chair or whatever, I'll let you challenge each other for positions. It's the way we run the Junior-Senior Band."

"What's that mean?" I asked.

"You can challenge the person who sits in front of you. For instance, Jeffi, if Norma decides she wants the first chair position, she challenges you."

"What do you have to do to challenge?" I don't know why I bothered to ask. I didn't have to challenge anyone and I certainly didn't want to give Norma any ideas.

"Play scales and sight-read a passage."

I looked at Norma sitting there head down, eyes on her lap. I couldn't imagine her having the nerve to challenge me. Even if she did, I could beat her hands down. But I still didn't like Mr. Bonner's idea very much.

As I walked through the lobby on my way to English the following period, I noticed the rain had started again. It was coming down in buckets. I'd probably need a boat to get home. The day got more depressing by the hour. I remember thinking, as I sat down in Miss Fuller's class, that nothing could make it worse.

I was wrong.

It was my turn to give my oral book report on *The Grapes of Wrath*. Despite all the hours of preparation and lost sleep, I was glad Miss Fuller had given the assignment. Speaking before a group was an important skill to develop if you wanted to be a lawyer, as I did. Besides, I enjoyed having people listen to my opinion.

I had just finished my first note card when Mr. Roscher, one of the guidance counselors, opened the classroom door. He didn't knock, which I thought was rude, especially since he could see me standing in front of the class. With him stood a boy who looked vaguely familiar.

"Please continue, Jennifer," Miss Fuller said as she went to see what he wanted. But by then my report was ruined. Naturally, everyone stopped listening to me and tried to eavesdrop on the conversation at the door.

Even from that first moment, I never had a chance against Kurt Erickson.

Miss Fuller stood next to the door with him until I finished my report, which I did quickly once I realized no one, not even Miss Fuller, heard a word I said. Seething inside, I returned to my seat and stuffed my note cards in my book. I hadn't mentioned a fraction of the information I'd prepared.

"Psst, Jeffi," whispered Bethany from two seats behind me. "That's the mysterious stranger."

I leaned around Butch Norcross's desk. "What stranger?"

"The boy at the mall."

Miss Fuller cleared her voice and I quickly turned around. "Class, this is Kurt Erickson. He just enrolled at Daniel Boone and will be in your section. I know you'll make him feel at home."

She could have saved her breath. From the way all the girls were gaping at him, I knew Kurt Erickson would have the full attention of at least half the class. By lunch, he was the hottest topic of the day.

"Kurt's fitting in already," Bethany said as we sat down at our table. "Look, he's sitting with Pete, John, and Warren."

I dug into my brown bag for something digestible.

"I think he's a doll," Sara added.

"Anyone want a liverwurst sandwich?"

"Those eyes! Have you ever seen anyone with such gorgeous eyes? They're like sapphires. I love them," cooed Bethany. "I noticed that about him when we met at the mall."

"Whatever happened to Frank's gorgeous eyes?" I bit into my apple.

"I'm only commenting, Jeffi. I can look, can't I?"

"Thank you for the commentary, Ms. Freedman. When are you going to get to the part about his flaxen hair, athletic body, and attractive facial features?"

"What's bugging her?" Bethany reached across the table to steal some corn chips from Sara.

"Who knows?" Sara replied. "But I'll tell you this. Kurt is the best thing that's happened to our class all year."

"Maryellen says he used to live in Spain. His father was in the State Department."

I stuffed the apple core in the bottom of my bag on top of the uneaten liverwurst. "How does she know?"

"She was in the office with the attendance sheet when he and his parents came in this morning."

"Señora Martinez will be overwhelmed with joy," I muttered.

Bethany twisted a strand of hair around her finger. "You know, girls, Kurt is definitely dating material. What do you think?"

"It would be a shame to waste him," said Sara.

They both looked at me.

"Forget it!" I said, crumpling up my bag.

"Don't get testy," said Bethany. "I guess he can't compare with Mike Hauser anyway."

The bell rang and we gathered up our books for the next class. Outside the biology room, Pete came up behind us. "Hey, you guys."

"We are *not* guys, Peter," Bethany said coolly.

"Excuse me. Girls. I want you to meet Kurt. This is Sara Herchek, Bethany Freedman, and Jeffi Anders."

"We met at the mall last Saturday," Bethany said in her sugar-and-honey voice.

Kurt nodded. "I thought you looked familiar."

"Hope you like it here." Sara smiled.

"I'm sure I will. Everyone has been very friendly so far," Kurt replied, looking at me. "I liked your book report, Jeffi. That's one of my favorite books. I bet your report convinced other kids to read it."

It might have if you hadn't barged in and interrupted, I thought. I forced myself to say, "Thanks."

Pete, Sara, and Bethany went into the classroom, leaving Kurt and me alone in the hall. I was trapped.

Kurt stepped closer. "Have you read any other Steinbeck books?"

"A few."

"Which ones?"

"We'd better go in before we're late," I said brusquely.

"Sure." He held the door for me. I brushed past him and hurried to my seat. I had the feeling this wasn't the last time Kurt Erickson would ruin a day for me.

By the end of the week, I would have done anything for a pair of earplugs. All anyone could talk about was "that cute Kurt Erickson." In P.E. on Wednesday, Mona Barnard informed the entire locker room that Kurt sat next to her on the bus and walked her from Spanish to English that morning.

"He's mine," she announced with her perky little nose in the air, "and nobody had better get in my way."

I wanted to say, "You can have him, Mona, dear," but I didn't. Why antagonize Dagger-in-the-Back Barnard?

When I wasn't hearing how many countries Kurt had lived in or what he ate for lunch, I was listening to Bethany's orations about Dyan's upcoming party.

"Everybody who's anybody will be there," she told Sara and me as we walked to algebra class. "And you know what Dyan's parties are like. My parents would die if they knew."

I'd heard whispers about wild parties, but I never learned exactly what went on at one. "What are they like?" I asked.

"Where have you been, Jeffi? Everybody knows about those parties, don't they, Sara?"

"Yes, I suppose so."

I didn't think either one of them knew much more than I did.

"I'll give you a full report Monday morning," Bethany said. "And, Jeffi, I'll tell you who Mike Hauser's date is."

Just what I wanted to hear. "Don't bother. I'm not interested in him any more."

"You're not giving up yet? These things take time."

"Beth's right," Sara chimed in. "He only noticed you were alive last week. You can't expect miracles."

A miracle is what I needed to get Mike's attention. Although he said "hi" to me a couple times since the dance, I knew it didn't mean much. He only did it because I was walking straight toward him. I wasn't as stupid as Mona Barnard who thought every breath a guy took in her presence had a mystical significance.

"I have better things to do than worry about Mike Hauser and the girl he takes to the Halloween party. I don't care if he's with Wonder Woman or Dracula."

All through *Night of the Living Dead*, I wondered what was going on at Dyan's party. By now, Mike and Wonder Woman were probably dancing cheek to cheek or huddled in a dark corner. Ugh! I didn't want to think about it!

Sara squeezed my arm.

"Not so hard," I whispered. "You'll leave your fingernails permanently embedded in my skin."

"It's so scary, I can't stand it!" She put her hands over her eyes. "Tell me when this part's over."

The library's public meeting room was jammed with kids seated on chairs and sprawled on the carpet. Because Sara and I arrived late, we were near the back. We found seats with a good view of the screen—which made no difference to Sara, who spent most of the movie with eyes closed.

"Wasn't that the best horror flick you ever saw?" she said as we walked down the front steps of the library.

"Did you *see* any of it?" I laughed. The cold air on my face felt good after two hours squeezed into a room with 100 screaming bodies. I wondered if Dyan's party were over yet. "What time is it?"

"Only ten. We have time to stop in The Alley. Anyway, I need to get my mind off that movie before we walk home."

The low, wooden-beamed ceiling and small windows of the basement soda shop made The Alley seem cozy and intimate. Tonight it was just plain crowded. All the booths along the walls were filled as were the round tables in the middle of the room. At first, I thought we'd have to sit at the counter, which I hate. It's too conspicuous. I feel as if everyone in the place will notice if I drop my fork or plop the catsup. Fortunately I spotted Pete sitting in a booth near the back. I caught his eye and he signaled us to join him.

"I saw you leaving the library," he said. "Great movie! I see it every Halloween. Here, Sara, next to me." He moved over.

"What's wrong with me, Pete? I have the plague?" I slid into the other bench.

"I've got a friend with me. You can sit with him."

Pete and Sara began talking about the movie and I tuned out. Did Mike meet Wonder Woman, whoever she was, at the party or did he pick her up like a real date? Did Dyan have the lights low and romantic?

Sometimes I can be pretty dense when I'm concentrating on other things. Still, I should have pieced it together when I saw Kurt come out of the men's room.

"Hi, Kurt," Sara said cheerfully when he came to our table.

"Hi." He looked at me as if he wanted to say something.

"Aren't you going to make room for Kurt to sit down?" Pete said, giving me a funny look.

That's when the light bulb went on in my head.

"Oh, sorry." I picked up my coat and stuffed it next to the wall. I moved over as far as possible. Kurt inched toward me until our shoulders and legs touched. If you ask me, it was closer than he had to be. Wow! If Mona saw this, she'd have a stroke.

"What do you think of the town so far?" asked Sara after the waiter took our order.

I felt Kurt's knee against mine. I couldn't decide whether I liked it or not, but there was no room to move even if I wanted to.

"I like it. Pete's been showing me around."

"Corrupting you, no doubt," I interjected.

"Maybe a little," joked Kurt, "but mostly we've been behaving."

"It must be boring to live here after being in Europe," Sara said.

Kurt's shoulder slid against mine as he shrugged. "Actually, I'm glad my Dad's staying put for awhile. I've been in a different school every two years since kindergarten."

"Kurt's father teaches political science at the university." Peter took his cola and cheeseburger off the waiter's tray.

"That's quite a way to commute," Sara said as she bit off the end of a French fry.

"My mother hates cities and wanted to live in a quiet little town, so here we are." Kurt pushed his blonde hair off his forehead. I noticed he had freckles. Kind of cute, if you like freckles.

"What'd you think of that quiz Terrible Trimble gave Friday?" Pete asked.

Sara rolled her eyes. "I absolutely hate algebra. If I see another x, y, or z, I'm going to be sick."

"It was tough, wasn't it?" Kurt said.

"You mean he made you take it even though you've only been here a few days?" Sara sounded as if she'd exposed a major injustice.

Serves him right for ruining my book report, I thought. But I said, "I don't think that's fair."

Kurt looked at me. Correction—he looked at my eyes. What's that expression about the eyes being the windows of the soul? It's true. Suddenly I felt very uncomfortable.

"It was fair. The quiz was on what we'd covered since I've been here. Anyway I was studying the same material at my old school."

I broke from his gaze and dipped a fry in the catsup.

"I hate having algebra after lunch." Pete reached across the table for the mustard. "Trimble smells worse than the locker room after the smoking crowd's been in there."

We all laughed.

"And how about when he leans over your desk to help you?" Sara added. "He must live on onions and garlic. I'm so busy holding my breath, I never hear a word he says to me."

"It's not that bad," I said.

"How would you know? He never needs to help you." Pete turned to Kurt. "In case you haven't already figured it out, Jeffi's our own Ms. Einstein."

What's Kurt going to say now? Is he the type who makes wisecracks about smart girls? Or will he be so intimidated he won't say anything at all?

"I thought you were good in math. The way you solved that homework problem Thursday was quite clever."

Clever? I never expected a comment like that. Why did he have to make it so hard to dislike him?

5

On Monday, Mr. Trimble returned our quizzes. I could have kicked myself for making a careless mistake that fouled up a whole problem and cost me 20 points. But after seeing the other kids' expressions, I was glad for the 80.

Mr. Trimble paced back and forth in front of his desk, shaking his grade book and stroking his mustache. Once I counted that he touched his mustache 118 times an hour. That's 1888 times a day, not counting the eight hours he slept. For all I know, maybe he strokes it then too.

"You people had better get it into your heads that we are involved in serious business in this class." His face looked like an overripe tomato bursting its skin. "Out of 25, only 2 people got a passing grade. Inexcusable!"

Only two! I must have made the best grade in the class, even if it was only an 80.

"Next week, I expect every one of you to pass the unit test. Everyone!" He raised his arm and threw a piece of chalk at the back wall. Tommy Jagger ducked just in time. "Now let's go over today's homework," Trimble said as he reached for a new piece of chalk. "By the way, Erickson, good job on the quiz."

Erickson?!

"I knew I was awful at algebra," moaned Sara on our way to history. "I'll be booted out of Honor Society if I don't do better in that class."

"Don't worry, Sara. It's just a quiz," I said. "I wonder how Bethany did."

"The way she had her mind on that party all day Friday, she probably did worse than I. She was smart to stay home today. I should have too. Mondays are bad enough without failing algebra quizzes."

"Speaking of the party, have you noticed that none of Dyan's crowd is in school today?" Including Mike.

"Really?" Sara replied as though she hadn't heard me. "Can you believe Kurt got 100 on the quiz? I saw his paper. He must be sharp."

"He had all that stuff at his old school."

Sara shook her head. "No, Jeffi, remember he said he was doing the same things. . . ."

"Forget it. It doesn't matter, does it?"

"I bet he's as good as you, maybe better."

"Must have been some party at Dyan's."

"Don't change the subject. You aren't afraid of a little competition, are you?"

"Maybe we should call Bethany."

"We'll hear about the party soon enough. Besides, we had as much fun as she did Halloween night." Sara hesitated. "Do you think it would be crazy if I made Pete Symons my Special Someone?"

"I thought I saw stars in your eyes."

Sara clutched her books close to her body. Her knuckles were white. "Don't tell Bethany yet. She thinks no guy is worth a dime if he isn't a jock."

"You agreed with her."

"But Pete is so, oh, you know, so down-to-earth. He listens when you talk. He doesn't think he's God's gift to women the way some guys do. You know what I mean?"

"Yeah, I guess so."

I learned my lesson about matchmaking in fifth grade when I tried to fix up Lina Swenson and Tommy Jagger. After a couple of weeks of taking messages between their desks and arranging "chance" meetings at recess, they both hated me and each other. So when Pete caught up with me on the way home, I kept my mouth shut about Sara.

"That was fun at The Alley, wasn't it?" He jumped up to snatch a solitary maple leaf dangling from a low-hanging branch.

"It was OK." I bet they did more interesting things at Dyan's party than sip sodas and discuss old horror movies.

"I enjoyed being with Sara." He twirled the yellow leaf between his fingers so fast it became a blur.

"Yeah?"

"Kurt's great too. I'm glad he moved here, aren't you?"

How could he ask that? The only time Mr. Trimble had ever complimented anyone in front of the class was when I solved three of his extra-credit brain teasers. Until Kurt came.

"Why do I get the feeling you don't like Kurt, good buddy?" He flipped the leaf in my face.

I pushed it away. "To tell the truth, I haven't given him any thought."

"I can't figure out why not. You two have a lot in common."

I walked on in silence. Pete got the message. He dropped the leaf into the gutter.

As we crossed the street in front of Old Man Harvey's house, he opened the door. He was usually stooped over as though he carried a rock on his back, but today he seemed more bent and crooked than ever. He wore wrinkled gray pants and his shabby-looking coat. Actually I'd never seen him wear anything else.

"You kids, come here!" Waving a broom, he hobbled to the edge of the porch.

Pete and I looked at each other, then walked slowly to the end of his sidewalk. I wasn't about to go any closer.

He squinted at us from behind his wire rims. "You know who did this to my porch last night?" The floor was covered with a thin layer of corn kernels. His front door had been bombarded with eggs, then foamed with shaving cream. By now, the coating was probably sealed to his door like cement.

"I didn't see anybody do it, Mr. Harvey," I replied.

"Any of your friends around last night?"

"None of our friends would do something like that, Mr. Harvey."

He started down the steps toward us. "If I ever find the kids who did this, they'll be sorry! That'll be the last time those hoodlums will bother me!"

Pete and I turned and ran.

"Boy, is he weird!" Pete said when we were safely in my yard.

"Why would he leave that mess on his porch all day? It was as if he wanted everyone to see it. The kids will never leave him alone now."

"He's asking for trouble, that's for sure," Pete said as Old Man Harvey retreated into his house. "And speaking of trouble, did you hear about the shake-up in the trumpet section?"

"Poor Ben. He's been first-chair trumpet for a long time."

"Ben's mistake was that he didn't think anyone could be better than he was."

"You're lucky you're the only tuba, Pete."

"If I were you, Jeffi, I'd watch out for Norma."

"I'm not worried. She's too mousy to challenge me."

"I hope you're right. People can surprise you."

I didn't realize then how right Pete was.

Sometimes I feel as if I'm floating in the ocean on a rubber raft. For awhile, I ride high on the crest of a teriffic wave. Then suddenly, the wave passes and I'm down in the trough. That's what November was like. Crests and troughs.

It all started during study hall on Thursday. Usually Sara, Bethany, and I sit in the back talking or doing homework together. But this time Sara went to the art room to finish a project and

Bethany wanted to write a note to Frank. Since Halloween, she had been totally wrapped up in him. At lunch, they sat together at the basketball table feeding each other French fries. It ruined my appetite to watch. Bethany said they were in love.

Since it was too noisy in study hall to study—Miss Longren doesn't care what you do as long as you stay in your seat—I went to the library to find a book for the next English oral report. I was browsing in the Ts when the wave caught me.

"Psst, Jeffi, over here."

Mike poked his head around the end of the bookcase. I almost dropped the book.

"When you're finished, come over here." His head disappeared.

I remained in the stacks for a few minutes, pretending to skim titles. I didn't want to appear too anxious. When I thought I'd been in there long enough, I grabbed a book and walked out as casually as I could. Under the circumstances, it wasn't easy! Mike sat at a study table. He pulled out the chair next to him and motioned for me to sit down.

Don't get nervous, I reminded myself. Don't let your mind go blank. Pretend you're talking to an ordinary guy. Forget he's anyone special.

"I've never seen you in here this period," he whispered.

"Study hall was boring today."

"Want some gum?"

"She'll kill us if she sees." I looked at Mrs. Prixer behind the check-out desk.

"Then don't let her see." He blew a bubble, then soundlessly sucked it back into his mouth.

Keeping my eyes on Mrs. Prixer, I unwrapped the gum in my lap and quickly popped it into my mouth. I watched Mike's jaw move up and down as he chewed. For the first time, I noticed that he shaved. I wonder if Bethany knew. That kind of thing really impressed her.

"Did you see the Mount Penn game?"

"Terrific game, Mike. You were great." I suppose he was because we won.

"Coach McNelly says I have a good chance at a football scholarship at State if I keep it up."

I didn't realize people worried about football scholarships in tenth grade. "I'm sure you will. You'll be even better next year."

"Look out. Prixer is giving us the hairy eyeball." I opened my book and Mike shuffled some papers. "It's clear now. She went in her office," Mike said a few minutes later. "Do you know much about math?"

I looked at the notebook in front of him. He had been working on algebra homework when I sat down, and his paper was covered with crossouts and erasures. "Are you having trouble?"

"Nah, this stuff's a breeze. It's just that I got a little behind. You know, with practices and all. And I missed class when he explained simultaneous equations."

"That's not hard. You try to get one of the variables to cancel out. Let me show you." I reached for his book and did one of the problems. "See what I mean?"

"I think so." He moved his chair closer. "I'll do one and you check me." His hand brushed mine as he turned the page. By the end of the period, we had finished Mike's homework and the fog had completely engulfed me.

"Thanks, Jeffi," Mike said when we left the library. "That had to be one of my more pleasant hours in Prixer's Tomb."

And it was THE most pleasant hour in my entire life!

The crest of that wave lasted until history class the following Monday when we met in our committees for the first time to discuss the presentations. Since mid-October when the groups were assigned, all the students were supposed to have been doing independent reading about their committees' topics. I figured only Mona and LuAnn would bother doing any preliminary work, so I made sure I read as much as I could. I already had ideas for our report.

"Remember, class," said Ms. Morgan before we broke into

groups. "Your job is to present an overview of one specific era of American history. My evaluation will be based on the accuracy of your information and how skillfully you summarize and organize."

My committee was assigned to the conference room next door. Mona, LuAnn, and I were spreading our notes on the table when Tommy Jagger and Butch Norcross came in and flopped down on the cushions against the wall.

"How did we get stuck with those goof-offs?" Mona whispered.

"I heard that," said Butch. "You should be glad to have us. Tommy and I are experts on the Civil War."

"Then why don't you sit at the table and contribute some of your vast knowledge to the discussion?" I opened my notebook.

They tossed their books onto the table and sat down. I could tell they were going to be two big pains in the neck.

"I have a few ideas on how to do this presentation," I began. "Anyone else have any suggestions?"

Before anybody could answer, there was a short knock on the door and Kurt Erickson stepped in. Why did he always barge in on me like that?

"Is this the Civil War committee?"

"Kurt!" said Mona breathlessly. "Are you in our group?" She picked her books off the chair beside her. How obvious can you get?

He nodded as he sat down next to her. "Ms. Morgan told me a few weeks ago so I could do the reading. I didn't know who else was on the committee. Go ahead, Jeffi. I'm sorry I interrupted."

"As I was saying." I cleared my voice. "Does anyone have suggestions on how to do this presentation?"

"I think we should tell about the battles," Butch said.

"Yeah, we could dress up like Yankee and Confederate soldiers. I have some fake blood at home for realism," Tommy added.

"That's *so* immature," sniffed Mona.

"I think we ought to concentrate on the causes of the war," I said. "Maybe illustrate each with a skit. Then discuss a few important battles and end with Lee handing over his sword to Grant."

"Grant let him keep his sword, stupid," snarled Butch.

"It's just symbolic, Butch. By the way, someone should be writing this down."

"I'll do it, Jeffi." LuAnn always volunteered to be secretary. I think she did it to avoid participating in the discussion.

We spent 15 minutes arguing about which battles to include. If we had used all the ones Butch wanted, our presentation would have taken two hours instead of 20 minutes. At last we agreed on four.

"Since you two are such experts on this, you write up the battle part of the report," I told Butch and Tommy. "And be sure to get the facts right." Knowing them, the rest of us would end up rewriting their part the day it was due.

"Don't worry!" Tommy gave me a dirty look.

"What about the causes?" LuAnn asked, starting a new page in her notes.

"I thought we could divide them up into words that start with *s*."

"Very clever," Butch snickered.

"Let Jeffi explain," Kurt said. It was the first time he had spoken.

"There's slavery, secession, states' rights, Stowe, and Sumter."

"What does Stowe have to do with anything?" challenged Tommy.

"If you read the assignment, you'd know I mean Harriet Beecher Stowe's book, *Uncle Tom's Cabin*. It had a lot to do with getting people angry about slavery."

"Ah, she wasn't that important. You're looking for an excuse to put a woman in this." Butch pointed his pen at me. "Just because Ms. Morgan made you committee head doesn't mean we have to do everything you want."

"What do you think, Mona?" I said, searching for an ally.

"Well, maybe. I don't know. I want to hear Kurt's opinion."

Everyone looked at Kurt. "I agree with Butch. Stowe's not important enough to include."

"I think Kurt is right," LuAnn chimed in. "Let's eliminate Stowe." I saw her smile at Kurt. She was lucky Mona didn't notice.

"Kurt has an excellent point," Mona quickly added.

"I'm the one who said it first!" cried Butch indignantly.

Sorry, Butch, but you don't have sapphire eyes and flaxen hair.

"Listen, you guys." I stood up. That gives you authority. "You know how Ms. Morgan always talks about the effect of literature on history. She'll love it if we include Stowe."

"There won't be enough time if we put in all the important things." Kurt stood up too.

"Give up, Jeffi. Nobody likes your idea." Tommy leaned his chair back on two legs. If only he'd lose his balance . . .

"Why couldn't we tie Stowe into the abolitionists and slavery?" I said staring directly at Kurt. "Those are main topics, right?"

"Yeah, but . . ."

"It only takes a minute to mention the effect of her book. This is the kind of thing Ms. Morgan wants. I'll write that part."

Kurt was silent for a minute. Then he sat down. "All right, I'll go along with that."

"So what?" Butch grumbled. "This should be democratic. I want a vote."

We voted and I won, four to two. Mona and LuAnn changed their minds and voted with me or, more accurately, with Kurt. I hate seeing intelligent girls act like airheads around a guy.

Every group meeting after that was a disaster. Butch and Tommy disagreed with anything I said, and Butch insisted we vote on each issue. LuAnn never opened her mouth except to agree with Kurt. And Mona acted as if her brain had turned to putty. She wouldn't take a stand until she heard Kurt's view.

Kurt—he'd ruined everything again. Unless I convinced him my ideas were better than Butch's, I lost the vote, five to one. Whenever he suggested something, no matter how dumb it was, I didn't have a chance because everybody voted with him. My dream of having the best presentation in the class rapidly slipped away.

By the week of Thanksgiving vacation, I was tired of fighting them. It was a relief to find my clarinet lesson scheduled for the same period as history. I knew they couldn't do anything drastic while I was gone since the only part left was tying together all the sections.

As I took my music from my locker, the wave came rolling down the hall. I felt my spirits lift as it approached.

"Haven't seen you much since that day in the library. How've you been?" Mike rested his elbow against the locker next to mine. I could smell his after-shave lotion. It was the same he'd worn the night of the dance.

"I've been around." I closed my locker.

"What class do you have next? I'll walk you there."

"I have to go all the way to the band room. You'll be late." Oh, why did I have to say that? Now he'll think I don't want him to walk with me.

"No problem. I have P.E., and Coach doesn't care if I'm a little late."

I couldn't believe it was happening. I was walking down the hall with Mike Hauser. Wait until Bethany and Sara heard!

Remember Bethany's advice: Keep talking, show him you're interested. "How did you do on your algebra homework?"

"Great. You're a terrific tutor."

Our bodies brushed together as we walked through the congested hallway. Why couldn't the band room be five miles away instead of around the next corner?

"Let me know if you ever want help again."

"Thanks, I will." His smile made my skin tingle. "Are you doing anything special over vacation?" he asked as we turned onto the band hall.

"Going to my cousins' for Thanksgiving Day. How about you?"

"My dad's taking me to the State game. We always go. My brother used to play for State, you know."

"Really?"

"We have super seats." His dark eyes danced. "Some day I'll be playing in a big game like that with thousands of people watching."

"Here's the band room. Thanks for walking me here."

"Hey, I enjoyed it." He waved as he headed down the hall. "See you later, Jeffi."

My heart was beating so hard I thought it would pop right out of my chest. When I opened the band room door, the other first clarinets were warming up and Mr. Bonner was sorting through music on his desk. Mike's voice floated around in my head. I hoped nobody talked to me for awhile so I could enjoy the memory. In biology or English class, I could dream about Mike the entire period and no one would notice. Unfortunately, you can't play a clarinet without concentrating. I had to shelve my thoughts for 50 minutes.

We spent the period practicing music for the Winter Holiday Assembly. It was an easy lesson since we played the songs every year. The Holiday Assembly is my favorite band performance because it's the only time we give a concert for the student body.

As I swabbed out my clarinet after the lesson, Norma approached me. "Jeffi, may I talk to you?" Her voice shook.

"Well, I'm sort of in a hurry." I placed my clarinet in its case. If I rushed, I'd have time to pass the gym and catch Mike leaving P.E.

Norma backed away. "I guess it can wait."

"Good, you can tell me later." I pushed my case into the storage closet and grabbed my books. I was almost out the door when Norma stopped me.

"No, I'd better tell you before vacation." She lowered her eyes. "Mr. Bonner says I have to tell you myself."

"Tell me what?"

The first time I didn't hear what she said because she mumbled. But there was no mistake when she repeated it.

"Please don't be mad, Jeffi."

"I'm not mad. You have the right to do it if you want." Who would have thought Norma had the nerve to challenge *me*?

"I'll probably lose anyway."

"I guess we'll find out, won't we?" I got away from Norma as fast as I could and went straight to English class. I didn't feel like seeing Mike any more.

Why did other people have to keep making problems for me? Just when things were developing with Mike, Norma had to come along and give me something to worry about. Why does my ocean have to be so choppy? I'm getting seasick.

6

Mr. Bonner scheduled Norma's challenge for the Tuesday after Thanksgiving vacation. "That gives you both a week to prepare your scales," he said.

I didn't need that long to prepare. I knew my scales, even the ones with four flats and sharps. On Monday night, I reviewed them all a couple of times and checked my reeds for a good one. I wasn't worried. I could finger faster than Norma any day.

"Your music sounded wonderful last night, Jennifer," Gram said as she cut my grapefruit Tuesday morning. Only Gram would call something as boring as scales wonderful. "Mr. Bonner must be a fine instructor to get you young people to practice so diligently."

I nodded and took a gulp of milk.

"Are you preparing for anything special, dear?"

I didn't see any reason to tell the world that Norma had challenged me. If I won, it wouldn't matter anyway. And if I lost . . . well, that wasn't going to happen. "We have the Holiday Assembly in two weeks," I replied.

"If this snow continues, we'll have a beautiful white Christmas," she said, looking out the window. "We haven't had snow this early in years. I wouldn't be surprised if we had a long, hard winter."

"It's only a couple of inches, Gram. It'll melt in a few days."

"Could be. Then again, have you noticed how the squirrels have been hoarding acorns all fall? They know they'll need more food than usual."

"I didn't notice."

"And the woolly caterpillars' coats. That's a sure sign. You wait and see if I'm not right, Jennifer."

Just what I needed: more time stuck inside my bulky sweaters.

It was torture waiting until after school for the challenge. Not that I was nervous—I just wanted to get it out of the way. I considered asking Mr. Bonner to change the time to before homeroom in the morning, but decided not to. I figured I could beat Norma no matter what time it was.

I didn't know about history class then.

Tuesday was the final day of committee meetings. Since I'd missed the last meeting, I hadn't seen the written reports. But the group had planned such silly skits that I knew we needed a terrific script in order to get a high grade.

"That sounds fairly good," I said after reading over the script in LuAnn's folder. Even Tommy and Butch had written a decent section. "And you guys wrote good transitions when I wasn't here too."

"We got along fine without you," Butch remarked snidely.

"Don't make it sound as if *you* helped, Butch," said Mona. "You and Tommy fooled around while the rest of us did all the work."

"We'd better decide who's going to play what parts in the skits, then we can practice," I said.

"I want to be Robert E. Lee," said Tommy. "I have a sword and Confederate hat at home."

"Better let him or he'll cry," said Mona.

I glanced over the list of skits. "Kurt should be Lincoln. He's the tallest."

"I can't, Jeffi. I'll be narrating."

"What do you mean? I'm the committee leader. I'm supposed to narrate."

There was a long silence.

"What's going on here? Mona? LuAnn?"

"Well, uh . . . Jeffi, we had a vote last time." Mona avoided looking at me. "And we decided Kurt had a better speaking voice than you."

"A guy makes a better narrator," added Butch.

"This was your idea, wasn't it, Butch?" I said angrily. "You're just an ignorant sexist. You hate the thought that a woman can do anything better than a man!"

"Don't get mad at Butch," Kurt said. "It was my idea. I wanted to narrate. I didn't realize you were planning on it."

Yeah, I bet.

The rest of the meeting was humiliating. I ended up being Lincoln because I was taller than LuAnn and Mona, and Butch was too fat. When the bell rang, I sat at the table until they all left. The last thing I wanted to do was listen to Mona and LuAnn swoon over Kurt while we walked down the hall.

"Jeffi?"

Startled, I swung around in my chair. Kurt stood in the doorway. He closed the door and sat down next to me. I didn't let myself look at him.

"I feel badly about the presentation. I didn't know you wanted to narrate."

"Forget it."

"Look, I'll let you do it, if you want."

"They voted for you. It's a democracy."

"But they didn't realize how much you wanted it." His voice was infuriatingly calm. I felt like screaming. "You deserve to be narrator," Kurt continued. "You put in more work than anyone in organizing the presentation. And I know Butch and Tommy didn't make it easy."

I spun around and glared at him. "Neither did you."

"What does that mean?"

"Always arguing with me. Disagreeing with every idea I had." My cheeks were on fire.

"Some of your ideas were good." Kurt frowned. "But what's wrong with disagreement and debate? I thought you liked that.

That's what lawyers do, isn't it?"

How did he know I planned to be a lawyer?

I gathered my books and stood up. "I have to go to my locker before Spanish. Let's drop it. You narrate and I'll be Honest Abe."

He followed me into the hall. "I'll walk you to your locker."

"Don't bother."

He grabbed my arm. "Come on, Jeffi. Can't we be friends?"

His hand burned through my sleeve as his eyes stared into mine. Suddenly, a feeling of confusion overwhelmed me. Pulling my arm away, I ran down the hall.

Part of me hated Kurt for all the things he had done to me since he came here. And yet, when he touched me, I felt something else. But what? I couldn't sort out my feelings for him. My head whirled and the muscles in my neck got tighter and tighter. I knew I had to concentrate on the challenge with Norma, but I couldn't get Kurt off my mind.

When the three-o'clock bell rang, I hurried to the band room. If I had a chance to practice before Norma arrived, I might be able to pull myself together. But she was already in the corner tuning her clarinet with the piano.

Mr. Bonner came out of his office with a cup of coffee and sat on his stool. I assembled my clarinet, picked up the reed I'd chosen the night before, and sat down next to him. Norma remained in her corner.

"Since this is Norma's challenge, I'll let her decide who will go first," Mr. Bonner said, sipping his coffee.

"I will," she said softly.

That was fine with me. I needed time to clear my mind.

"I'll ask each of you to play three scales, then sight-read a passage. Understood?"

We both nodded.

"Take a couple of minutes to warm up. Then Jeffi can wait in my office while Norma plays."

I ran up and down the chromatic and practiced a few scales until Mr. Bonner signaled us to stop. Before I went in his office, I stopped at the piano. "Good luck, Norma."

"You, too," she murmured, staring at the floor.

That's when I noticed her hands. Norma had cut her nails! And they were shorter than mine. I couldn't take my eyes off them.

"Something wrong, Jeffi?" Mr. Bonner asked.

"No." I walked slowly to his office. As I closed the door, I heard Norma and Mr. Bonner mumbling outside. Then she started a scale.

Norma cut her nails.

Concentrate on the A-flat scale. That's the hardest. Forget about everything else. Let the fingers take over.

Don't listen to Norma. She's not playing fast. You're imagining it. Calm down.

Scales . . . nails. Concentrate . . . narrate. First . . . Kurt. Fast . . . last.

Don't forget the rests when you sight-read.

Eighth notes . . . they're all dopes.

Now she's sight-reading. Ha! Hear that mistake? She's not so good. Just relax. That's the key.

Be sure to check the key signatures.

She stopped playing.

Stop your hands from shaking.

Norma was swabbing her clarinet when I came out. "You wait in my office, Norma, while Jeffi defends her chair," said Mr. Bonner.

"I'll be happy to, Mr. Bonner. Just call me when you're ready." It was the first time I'd heard Norma say two sentences in a row!

Let your fingers take over.

"Play the A scale first," Mr. Bonner said as he leaned against the chair next to me.

Three sharps. F, C, G. Fingers, go fast. A, B, C♯, D, E, F—oops—F♯, G♯, A, B, C—oops—C♯, D . . . Oh no! My fingers aren't working. Scales. Nails. Is Norma listening?

I went through three octaves of the scale and made five mistakes. Then the E-flat scale—six mistakes. By the time Mr. Bonner put a sheet of sight-reading music in front of me, my fingers were numb!

The notes danced all over the page.

I didn't cry. Not when Norma came out of the office smiling. Not when Mr. Bonner said I could challenge her later if I wanted. Not on the way home when some dumb jerk drove by and splashed sloshy snow all over my suede coat. Not when Gram told me it was my own fault for wearing a suede coat on a wet day. Not when Ralph yelled at me for being late. Not when Mom sent me to my room in the middle of dinner because I let a "shocking" word escape when Ralph pushed me too far. And not even when Mom sat on the edge of my bed and asked me what was wrong.

"Nothing's wrong," I said, keeping my back to her.

"Jennifer, I know you well enough to recognize when things aren't right. Ever since you came home, your behavior has been outrageous. Did something happen today at school?"

She'd never understand.

"Nothing happened. Everything's great at school."

"Jennifer, what's going on?"

I just wanted to be left alone, but I could tell Mom would be planted on the edge of my bed until I told her something, anything. I jumped off the bed and faced her. "I'm sick and tired of being treated like a child around here!" I shouted. For a second, I was shocked at how angry I sounded. I wasn't even trying. "Ralph makes me feel like a baby. Always nagging me, yelling at me, never listening to my opinion. I'm almost 16. In some societies, I'd be considered an adult!"

Mom was silent for what seemed hours. Finally she stood up and smoothed her skirt. "I'm sorry you feel that way, Jennifer. Perhaps we can find a solution to the problem."

Oh no! I wanted to get her out of here. She's going to make a major issue out of this.

"I've always felt the first step toward being treated as an adult was accepting responsibilities."

Here it comes. The pull-your-own-weight lecture.

"Maybe if you took on more adult responsibilities, you could make that big step."

She stared at me until I said it. "Like what?"

"Well, it just so happens that Ralph needs help in his office. His former secretary made a shambles of the files. The woman he recently hired doesn't have time to straighten them out and do the daily work, too. And you know how impossible it is to run an office with a bad filing system."

"I don't see how I . . . "

"I'm sure if you offered to help Ralph, it would go a long way toward earning his respect." She walked toward the door. "Why don't you talk to him tomorrow?"

I was trapped. "OK," I said, nodding. All I wanted was to stop her prying. Now I was stuck working for Ralph. Nothing had turned out the way it was supposed to.

I opened my closet door. The box was way in the back. I hadn't had it out in ages, but I knew she'd be there. I took the top off and felt around until I touched the silky hair and soft cotton dress. Holding her close, I climbed into bed. Her plastic smell reminded me of days when my biggest problem had been tying my shoes. I pulled the covers over my head and rested my cheek against her hair.

That's when I cried.

Working in Ralph's office turned out not to be so bad. For one thing, neither Ralph nor Paula, his new secretary, tried to boss me around. The first afternoon, Paula put a table and chair in the file room, wished me luck, and returned to her desk. I think she was so disgusted with the files that she didn't care what I did. Ralph seemed grateful just to have someone willing to tackle the job.

Mom expected me to work for free, but I made it clear to Ralph from the beginning that my time was valuable.

"I can't afford to pay you much, Jeffi. How about two dollars an hour?"

I was surprised that Mr. Tight-Fist would offer to pay that much. Especially since he could have had me for nothing if Mom had been involved in our agreement. "You'd have to pay a secretary at least twice that," I said indignantly.

"I'm sorry. But that's why I need your help. I can't spare the extra money to hire someone at minimum wage."

"You make plenty from your patients."

Ralph's forehead wrinkled up. "I have thousands of dollars wrapped up in my equipment and office rent. Not to mention paying off my loans from college." He looked at me hard for a minute. "Forget it. That's not your problem. I'd pay you more if I could, but I'm afraid two bucks is the limit."

I actually felt sorry for him. I decided I could be satisfied with two dollars an hour. It was more than I could make babysitting for the Donnellys, and it beat picking modeling clay out of a shag rug.

After an hour of checking names on the folders, I saw how big a mess the files were. Although some files were in the correct place, I found almost as many stuck under the wrong letter. The best way to fix it was to take them all out and refile. Fortunately, Ralph had only been practicing a couple of years and didn't have too many patients yet.

By the third afternoon, I'd developed a system using three-by-five cards with letters on them to keep all the files organized as I sorted through them. I started playing mental games to remember where I'd seen a certain name. For instance, Adamson, Ronald, was under Q—Q for John Quincy Adams, John Adams' son. Adamson. Maybe Ralph's secretary played the same sort of games, too, and that was why no one could decipher her filing system.

The best part of the job was having something to think about besides school. The first Saturday morning, I worked on the files for three hours and never once thought about Norma's fingers flying up her clarinet. Or about Kurt in front of the class narrating while I was hidden behind a fake beard and stovepipe hat. Or about Mike Hauser not paying me the least attention since the day he walked me to my clarinet lesson.

Right after lunch, Paula stuck her head around the corner of the file room. "Jeffi, have you come across Mr. Mowrey's file yet? The waiting room is jammed and I don't have time to root around for it. Who knows where I'd find it!"

"I'll try, but I've only refiled up to *D*. What's the first name?"

"Victor." Paula disappeared.

I checked under *M* in the shelves with no luck. It must have been filed incorrectly. I checked to see if it was in one of the piles I'd made on the floor. No again. I hadn't pulled it yet. I tried to remember if I had seen it when I thumbed through the files the first day.

It hit me like a flash of lightning! That's what's so exciting about using association to remember things. Once you recall one word, the whole thing unravels and you solve the problem instantly.

Victor Mowrey, V.M. Vroom. Race cars. Indy 500. *I*.

I thumbed through the *I* files on the shelf. There it was. Pulling the file, I hurried out to Paula's desk.

"Thank goodness you found it!" Paula looked frazzled. The hair in her twist stuck out in all directions and perspiration stains showed under the arms of her blouse.

"Is there something else I can do to help, Paula?"

"Sure you don't mind?"

Before I could answer, she handed me a blank patient chart. "I'll handle Mr. Mowrey. You take care of Mrs. Ziegler. She's new. Fill out the top of the chart."

Paula swirled around in her chair and started typing a mile a minute. I opened the door to the waiting room and called in Mrs. Ziegler. She was a plump, gray-haired woman who wobbled when she walked. As I helped her sit down in the chair next to the desk, she smiled at me the way all the sweet old ladies do when they see me in church.

"We'll fill out this form before you see the doctor," I said. "This is your first visit?"

"Oh, yes. My daughter suggested I come. I've gone to Dr. Howard all these years, but he's become so greedy. And on my social security, I couldn't afford his fees any more." She patted the worn-out leather purse on her lap.

"Full name, please."

"Mary Ziegler. And another thing. Dr. Howard's hours were so unreasonable. And he was always flying off to the Bahamas or somewhere. Now what is an old woman going to do when her glasses break and she needs them fixed right away?"

"Address?"

"144 Spring Street. Dr. Howard was so undependable. Not Dr. Anders though. He'll go out of his way for you."

"Phone number?"

"It's 948-7892. One time my little grandson, Timmy—he's only seven—broke his glasses in the schoolyard. You know how boys are. It was Friday afternoon. And you know, Dr. Anders stayed late in his office until Louie—that's my son-in-law—could get little Timmy over here. I ask you, how many doctors would do that?"

Paula rushed by. I gave her a pleading look but she ignored me. I was on my own. "Mrs. Ziegler, we must finish this so you can be examined."

"I guess I rambled on. I do that sometimes." She pulled the hem of her dress over her knees.

By the time I'd finally filled out the form, Paula returned. "He's ready for Mrs. Ziegler now. Why don't you show her back to the examining room, Jeffi?"

I helped her from the chair and she wobbled down the short hall behind me. When we reached the examination room, Ralph came to the door. "You must be Mrs. Ziegler? I hear you make the best oatmeal cookies in town. That true?" He gently took her arm and led her to the examining chair.

"Now who would say a thing like that?" Mrs. Ziegler giggled like a little girl.

"A real expert."

"Oh, you mean Timmy." Her face glowed. "My daughter didn't tell me how handsome you are, Dr. Anders."

"That proves it. You *do* need an eye examination." Ralph laughed. "Just relax, Mrs. Ziegler, and I'll see what I can do for you."

I thought I was listening to a stranger. I couldn't believe this was my grouchy, egocentric brother.

"Mrs. Ziegler wouldn't shut up about Ralph," I said to Paula when I came back to her desk. "You'd think he was the only decent eye doctor in the world."

"Lots of his patients feel that way." Paula put a sheet of paper in the typewriter. "And they must be telling their friends because we get new patients every week." She motioned toward the file room. "That's why we need those straightened out as soon as possible."

"I can take a hint." I went back to my piles of files.

By four o'clock, Ralph had seen the last patient and was ready to lock up. "I didn't know you saw so many people each day," I said as we drove home.

"Saturday's the only day some people can come so it's quite busy. Paula says you're doing a good job, Jeffi. If you can finish by Christmas, I'll be able to start the new year fresh."

"I think I can do that."

"Good." He switched on the radio.

"I never knew exactly what you did before, Ralph. It's interesting."

He looked across the seat at me. "Well, maybe some day you'll want to be my partner. You'd be good at it the way you like science."

I didn't want to hurt his feelings, but if I had to go to school all those years, I'd rather do something more exciting than examining retinas. "I want to be a lawyer."

Ralph laughed. "That's all right. I can use one of them, too."

How could I have lived with my brother so long and never seen this side of him? Maybe I'd been wrong about Ralph.

7

The Snowflake Dance posters appeared the second week in December. This year, the junior class was sponsoring it and they obviously weren't well-organized. I suppose it didn't matter that they forgot to advertise until the week before the dance. Everyone's calendar had had the date marked on it for months.

"Mother and I went shopping over the weekend and I bought the most spectacular dress for the dance," Bethany said, putting her tray down next to mine. Hook-shot Frank had left school early for an away game and she was eating lunch with Sara and me. "Only nine more days. I can hardly wait!"

"Do you want your pickles, Beth?" asked Sara.

Bethany dropped the dill slices on Sara's tray. "I heard that lots of guys are going stag. Don't you think that's awful? This is the biggest dance of the year next to the prom."

"Maybe they like playing the field," said Sara around a mouthful of pickle.

"It's better for unattached girls like me to have extra guys at the dance," I added.

"Jeffi, you don't have to go alone. Frank could set you up with Mike. He told Frank he thinks you're nice."

"He did? Really?" Sara put down her grilled cheese. "Wow, Jeffi! Didn't we tell you Mike liked you?"

I would have felt excitement, too, but I knew Bethany too well. "You asked Frank to ask Mike if he thought I was nice, didn't you?"

Bethany clicked her fingernails on her soda can. "What difference does it make how it happened? The point is he said it."

"If Mike Hauser wants to ask me, which I doubt, I want him to do it without prompting from anyone."

"It's up to you," replied Bethany, "but I know for a fact that he isn't involved with anyone else right now. Just think. We could all triple-date."

"Who asked you, Sara?" I said.

"No one yet." She shot me a please-drop-the-subject look. Did this have something to do with Pete?

"Don't worry, Sara," Bethany said reassuringly. "You'll get invited. There must be six guys in our section alone who adore you."

I had a feeling Sara only cared about one of them.

"I'm glad those history presentations are over," Sara said quickly. "I hope I never see another word about the Roaring Twenties!"

"The Civil War group was the best," Bethany remarked. Sara nodded in agreement.

I had to admit the whole thing turned out better than I had expected. Kurt did a fairly good job narrating although I would have done even better. At least Ms. Morgan gave us an A.

"Brilliant idea to put Harriet Beecher Stowe in," said Bethany. "My mother would salute you. She says women are always overlooked in history."

"I had to fight tooth and nail for that part. You know how moronic some guys can be."

"Did you see how Mona never took her eyes off Kurt through the entire presentation?" Bethany giggled. "I think she'll die if he doesn't ask her to the Snowflake Dance."

Suddenly the muscles in my neck tightened. I don't know why. I didn't care about Mona and Kurt. Or did I? "It's disgusting the way Mona chases after him."

"If you ask me," commented Sara as the bell rang, "Mona doesn't stand a chance."

"He could have his choice of girls," Bethany said as we put our trays on the cleanup cart.

"One thing for sure, he doesn't seem interested in anyone who's after him." Sara turned toward me, her eyes twinkling. I was supposed to know what she meant. I didn't.

We fought our way out of the cafeteria as the freshmen rushed in. "I think Kurt has a girl friend somewhere," said Bethany. "Why else would such a cute guy ignore all the girls who are dying to date him? What do you think, Jeffi?"

"How should I know?"

"You always get so uppity about him," she sniffed. "You're probably the only person in the class who doesn't like Kurt."

"Who said I didn't like him?"

"Well, do you?" asked Sara.

"I never think about Kurt one way or the other." But although I wouldn't dare admit it to them, I was thinking about him more and more.

The next day was the Winter Holiday Assembly. No one in band has said much after our challenge. Maybe they were all worried about keeping their own seats. The more I thought about it, the more I hated Mr. Bonner's challenge idea. Not just because of Norma and me, but because it made everybody in band too competitive. It wasn't fun any more.

The assembly wasn't fun either. I didn't have the warm holiday feeling I used to get when we played the carols. And instead of feeling proud of being onstage, I prayed nobody would notice that Jeffi Anders wasn't first-chair clarinet any more. I was glad when the final curtain closed.

After school, Sara and I planned to watch her cousin Sam in the wrestling match. I had spent all my free afternoons for the past couple of weeks in Ralph's office and I needed a break. Besides, I was all the way to the *T*'s and would finish the files long before vacation started.

I got to Sara's locker at three to wait for her. She was 15 minutes late. "Where were you? I've been waiting."

Sara pulled out her coat and books. "I was fixing my hair."

"For a wrestling match? You better not get as fussy as Bethany. I don't know if I can stand two of you at once."

"It's for Pete," she blurted out.

"Why didn't you tell me you were meeting him?"

"I didn't have a chance."

This was quite a switch for Sara. She rarely became serious about a guy, yet this thing with Pete had been going on since Halloween. The wrestling match had already started when we arrived, but Pete was waiting in front of the gym door for us. As we went inside, he took Sara's hand.

I was amazed so many people had come out for the match. Basketball was the big winter sport at Daniel Boone, but evidently the wrestling team had a faithful following too. The air in the gym was warm and dank with the smell of perspiration.

Sam started his match soon after we found seats. Sara practically knocked Pete and me out of the bleachers with her cheering. Sam was better than his opponent and pinned him in a few minutes. After his match, we spent more time talking than watching the wrestlers. Actually Sara and Pete talked and held hands. I sat there feeling like a third wheel. The way things were going, I'd be an old woman before a boy held my hand.

"I should get going, Sara," I said after I couldn't stand watching the lovebirds any more.

"No, don't, Jeffi. It's still early. And you and I were going to walk home together," Sara protested.

"Pete can walk you home."

Pete blushed. "I can't. My father's picking me up here later."

"Stay awhile longer, Jeffi. I don't want to leave yet." Sara rested her head on Pete's shoulder. "We've been terrible, Pete. Sitting here talking and not including Jeffi."

"You're right." Pete leaned around Sara. "That concert was one of our best, don't you think? Bonner seemed pleased."

"I enjoyed it," added Sara. "How come you and Norma switched seats this year, Jeffi?"

"I felt my face reddening. Pete jabbed Sara with his elbow.

"Oh, I'm sorry. I didn't know." Sara covered her mouth.

"It's no big deal. I had a bad day and Norma beat me, that's all. I was so busy with the history project that week, I just didn't have time to practice. I'll get my seat back. No problem."

"You'd better think about challenging her before the Spring Concert," said Pete. "That's when it really matters who's first chair."

He was right. Mom, Gram, and Ralph would be at that concert.

"I probably shouldn't say this," Sara said slowly, "but in a way, it's sort of nice for Norma to be first chair for awhile. She's not good at anything else. Not like you are, Jeffi."

"Thanks a lot, friend," I snapped. "And for your information, she's not so hot on the clarinet either. You should have heard her mistakes today. And the way she taps her foot . . . I think she's too stupid to count in her head like we're supposed to."

Sara gasped. "Jennifer Anders, I never heard you call anyone stupid before."

I don't know what made me say those things, but suddenly I wanted to escape. "I need fresh air. This gym is making me sick. I'll meet you outside."

The lobby was empty except for four or five kids milling around. I looked for a water fountain, but a couple was standing in front of it with their arms intertwined and their faces so close you couldn't slip a piece of paper between them. I decided I wasn't thirsty any more.

For lack of anything better to do, I walked over to the showcase along the wall. Inside were clay sculptures and pottery made by the art students. One grotesque figure with long, bony fingers reminded me of Norma. As I turned to peer into the next showcase, a gray sweat suit walked across the lobby from the locker rooms. My stomach somersaulted. Mike Hauser.

Should I call to him? Should I pretend I didn't notice him and see whether he speaks to me first? But what if he doesn't? If I don't change the way my life's going, I'll be the only single in a world of couples. He *did* say I was nice, didn't he? Be aggressive. That's the way to get a guy.

"Mike!" I called across the lobby. Two of the seniors near the door glanced at me, but Mike didn't turn around. "Mike!" I repeated louder.

"How you doing?" He flashed that famous Hauser smile. Instantly I felt gorgeous and glowing. It was as if he'd waved a magic wand over me.

"Fine. I was waiting for Sara. We came to see Sam wrestle."

"Oh." He shifted his bag to the other hand.

"Did you see him?"

"Uh, no. I was working out in the weight room." His eyes darted around the lobby.

"How are you doing in algebra now?"

His face was blank.

"You know. In the library a few weeks ago. I helped you."

"Oh, yeah," he said finally. "I'm doing fine, real fine." He smiled at me again. I melted.

Silence. Why couldn't I think of anything to say? Mike had a faraway look in his eyes. If only I could read his mind.

Finally he spoke. "You going to the dance?"

My heart started hammering. "Probably."

"Promise you'll save me a dance?"

"Sure." I tried to sound cool and collected. He hadn't asked me to go with him, but this was better than nothing.

"Good. You're really a smart girl. I appreciated your helping me that time in algebra."

"Anytime I can help again, let me know."

"Well, now that you mention it, I was just thinking maybe after vacation, we could work together more regularly. After school or something. It's more fun to study with someone else, right?"

My blood pressure rose above the danger point. "Oh, sure. Algebra's so boring otherwise."

"It's a deal then?"

"Deal."

He waved to me as his bus pulled up outside. The fog rolled in again. I couldn't wait to tell Sara.

"Mike wants us to do homework together after school," I told her after she and Pete had said good-bye. "I'm sure it's only an excuse to be with me because he said algebra was easy for him."

"You had to help him before, didn't you?" Sara said as we crossed the parking lot.

"That was during football season when he was busy with practice. This is the best thing that's ever happened. Bethany was right about everything. He does like me. Her advice worked."

"That's wonderful, Jeffi." She sounded like she couldn't care less.

"He wants me to save a dance for him. It's not as good as if he were taking me, but I'm not complaining."

Suddenly, Sara burst into tears.

"What's wrong with you?"

"Pete asked me if I would be at the dance," she sobbed.

"So why the tears? Maybe he likes going stag."

"No, no. That's not it. I . . . I can't go." Tears streamed down her cheeks.

"Why not?"

"Daddy was laid off at the knitting mill," she cried as we passed the junior high playing fields. Sara sat down on the bleachers. "I didn't want anyone to know, Jeffi."

"Your mother still has her job, doesn't she?"

"Yeah, but with only one pay check, there won't be money for extras." She put her head in her hands. "I couldn't ask them to buy me a new dress or even for the money to get in the dance."

"What about your baby-sitting money?" I wanted her to stop crying.

"I already used it on Christmas presents."

"If Pete knew, he'd pay your way."

"If he wanted to pay for me, he'd have asked me to go with him," she sniffled.

"I don't see why the mill's laying off. People always need

underwear."

"It has something to do with the economy. I don't understand all that." She rooted in her purse for a tissue. "You're lucky your brother's doing well."

"Ralph worries about money."

"Be glad he has some to worry about."

What did she expect me to do? It wasn't my fault the mill had laid off her father. Finally something exciting had happened to me, and Sara was so wrapped up in her own problems that she didn't even care. Some friend she turned out to be!

On Saturday, I worked in Ralph's office all morning. After lunch, I called Bethany to see if she'd help me find a dress for the dance. Bethany never turned down a shopping trip.

When I saw the deep-blue velveteen with lace cuffs and collar, I knew I had to have it.

"Mike's eyes will pop out when he sees you in this," Bethany said as I twirled around in front of the dressing room mirror. "With your hair pulled up, he won't be able to resist!"

"I hope you're right. But this dress costs almost twice what Mom gave me."

"Don't you have any money of your own?"

"Sure, but I planned to use it for a new clarinet case."

Bethany clicked her tongue. "It's up to you. Hook the neatest guy in school or lug around a new clarinet case."

As I looked at my reflection, I knew no other dress would satisfy me. I felt like Cinderella at the ball. The case could wait. Mike might not.

All week I was in heaven. Even Sara's moping couldn't ruin my mood. The dance would be wonderful. Nothing could possibly spoil it for me.

I hadn't counted on a blizzard.

When I awoke the morning of the Snowflake Dance, there was already six inches of snow on the ground. Despite its name, this was overdoing it! By noon, the snow was a foot deep and the dance was canceled. It wasn't fair!

On Monday, the whole school was in a blue funk. And why not? It had snowed long enough to cancel the dance and stopped in time for the roads to be opened for school. As if that weren't enough, I had P.E. first period. I dropped my books on the bench next to Bethany. She mumbled as she tied her sneakers.

"Talking to yourself again?"

"This darned snow! I hate it!"

"Join the club." I took my gym suit out of my locker. "Phew! I forgot to get this washed last week. Do you have any cologne I could spray on it?"

"No, sorry." Bethany slammed her locker door. "You'd think Miss Hovey would go easy on us this week. What a crab! Basketball again."

"I thought you were basketball's greatest fan?"

"Only if I'm not the one playing."

As I snapped up my gym suit, Mona and Sara entered the locker room. Mona's mouth was going full speed and, for the first time in more than a week, Sara was smiling. *She's glad the dance was canceled and we're all miserable*, I thought.

"Hi, you two," Mona bubbled. "Stop looking so glum. Mona's here to save the day."

"Hurry and tell them," Sara giggled.

"Yuk, what smells?" Mona pinched her nose.

"My gym suit. It's been fermenting in my locker since last Monday. Have any cologne?"

"No, and try to stay a polite distance away, will you?" Mona made a face.

"Tell them, Mona!" Sara hopped up and down off the bench like a five-year old waiting to see Santa Claus.

"Because I was so depressed about the dance's having been canceled," Mona said when she was sure we were giving her our undivided attention, "my parents said I could have a New Year's Eve party. It's only for our section to keep the size down. But, Bethany, you can bring Frank since you guys are practically engaged."

I wished I could bring somebody too. But then, I'm not "practically engaged." Probably never will be. I wouldn't have the nerve to ask Mike anyway.

"Of course, it won't be on New Year's Eve because my parents already planned to go out then. It'll be the night before."

"Isn't that terrific?" squealed Sara.

"Can you come?" Mona asked.

"I'll have to check with my mother," I replied. I knew Mom would say I could go. She and Mrs. Barnard played bridge together and Mom always said she wished Mona and I would become better friends. Fat chance.

"I'll let you know tomorrow," said Bethany. I could tell by her voice that she had no intention of going.

"I want to tell the other girls before Miss Hovey blows the whistle. Oh, I almost forgot. It's dressy. Like the Christmas dance." Mona flitted away.

Sara's smile suddenly faded. Lips quivering, she sat down on the bench.

Bethany put her arm around Sara's shoulders. "You can borrow my dress. I won't be using it now, thanks to the blizzard." I realized Bethany knew about Sara's father's being laid off too.

"You'll want it for Mona's party, won't you?" asked Sara.

"Frank's family is going to Florida for the vacation. I don't want to go to a party without him."

"Come on, Beth," I said. "I'm going even though Mike won't be there."

"That's different, Jeffi."

"Are you sure you don't mind if I borrow it?" Sara wiped away the solitary tear trickling down her cheek. "It was your special dress."

"Now it'll be special for you, too."

Vacation was an endless string of ancient relatives, turkey leftovers, and boring television. Mona's party couldn't compare with the Snowflake Dance, but it was better than sitting home another evening. Besides, I couldn't wait to show off my new dress, even if Prince Charming wouldn't see it.

The party was in the basement family room. I'd been there for birthday parties, but this time Mona and her mother had gone overboard with decorations. Red-and-green streamers and evergreen wreaths hung from the ceiling and walls. A Christmas tree in the corner was covered with twinkle lights and scores of hand-carved ornaments. No matter where you stood, there was a dish of peanuts, candies, or chips within easy reach. And a big tub of ice filled with sodas sat in the corner.

Sara nudged me as I popped some peanuts into my mouth. "You realize the reason for all this fuss, don't you?"

"No."

"Take a look."

I followed her gaze toward the steps. A smiling Mona in her floor-length hostess skirt was leading Kurt Erickson down the stairs.

"Watch out for the mistletoe, Kurt!" Butch shouted.

Kurt glanced over his head and quickly stepped aside. Mona shot a dirty look in Butch's direction.

"Better luck next time, Mona!" someone called out. Sara and I giggled.

Pete and the others arrived soon. Everybody had dressed up, even Butch and Tommy, just as they would have for the Snowflake Dance. Maybe it wasn't Cinderella's Ball, but I felt like her in my new dress. Bethany was right. It was better than a clarinet case.

"I want everyone to mingle," Mona said as she took a bunch of cards and a roll of masking tape from the table. "So I've planned a little activity."

I'd forgotten how Mona loved "little activities." I bet they didn't do things like that at Dyan Warren's parties.

"I'll put a name tag on everyone's back. It's the name of a famous person who has a connection to you. The object is to guess who your mystery person is."

Tommy Jagger made a wisecrack, which I couldn't quite hear. Mona glared at him. "You get clues by asking people yes-or-no questions. But you can only ask one question per person. That's how I get you to mingle." She smiled smugly. "The last person to guess helps me with the food.

"Am I man or woman?" Sara turned her back toward me.

"It has to be yes or no."

"Oh, right. Am I a woman?"

Her tag said "Pete Symons." Cute. I bet Pete's said "Sara Herchek." "No, not a woman. How about me? Female?"

"Nope."

After five questions, I'd learned I was a dead American male with a beard who lived more than a 100 years ago. That's when Kurt came over. *I'll try to get along with him tonight*, I thought. The way Cinderella would.

"I'm not very good at these kinds of games," he said.

I looked at his tag. Robert Redford. "What do you know so far?

"I'm an actor and director, still alive, have blond hair. It's hard to think of yes/no questions to narrow it down." He leaned close to me. "Would it be cheating if you gave me a clue? I'll give you one, too, if you want."

"Afraid of losing, Kurt?"

"Afraid of the consolation prize, that's all."

"Carrying a little food won't hurt you."

"But the mistletoe over the staircase might." He rolled his eyes.

I giggled. How Mona would hate it if we cheated at her game! "Why not? I love conspiracies, *Sundance Kid*, " I whispered.

"Robert Redford? Why did Mona give me that one?"

"Well, you do look a little like him."

"You're not going to like Mona's choice for you, Jeffi. But it *is* funny," he said looking at my back. "You were assassinated."

"Of course. Abe Lincoln! I don't think that's funny at all." But a second later, I was laughing with him.

LuAnn was the last to guess. Poor Mona. She'd counted on being huddled in the kitchen with Kurt. Maybe I shouldn't have sabotaged her plans.

Mona and her mother went all-out on food. There were little

sandwiches with the crusts cut off, carrot and celery sticks, rolls and cold cuts. I only took a few carrots and a small cucumber sandwich. I'd eaten so many peanuts I could feel my body manufacturing fat. Then LuAnn came down with a scrumptious-looking cheesecake and instantly I gave up the plan to be nutrition conscious.

After we'd eaten, Mona took out another stack of cards and announced a dance contest. She quickly grabbed Kurt as her partner. She wasn't taking any more chances. Everyone else paired up. Butch asked me. He had some nerve after the way he'd treated me during our history project! I said OK anyway. Tommy Jagger was left over and volunteered to run the contest.

We danced for several minutes, then Tommy stopped the music. "If the girl has on a ring, you're eliminated," he read from one of the cards in Mona's stack. A few couples dropped out.

The music continued. Butch smelled like onions. "If the boy has on a brown belt, sit down." Butch was too fat to need one.

At last we were eliminated on "either person wearing a watch." I was glad I'd worn mine, otherwise I would have been stuck with Butch even longer. After a few more cards, Sara and Pete were the only ones left. Mona gave them gift certificates for The Alley.

Once the dance contest ended, someone turned the lights down. Mona closed the door to upstairs, LuAnn put a slow record on the stereo, and a few couples began dancing again. Sara and Pete disappeared into a dark corner under the steps.

In such a romantic atmosphere, I felt conspicuous standing by myself. I considered going over to the sofa where Mona, LuAnn, and the other unattached girls were clustered trying to get the boys to dance with them. But the last thing I wanted was Butch Norcross breathing onions on me again.

Some of the guys stood around the food table stuffing their faces. They looked as uncomfortable as I felt. Maybe eating the night away wasn't a bad strategy though. I parked myself in a chair next to the avocado dip and dug in. I was munching a bunch of Fritos when it happened.

"I'd like to dance with you." Kurt smiled and brushed the hair off his forehead.

Was he asking or telling? "Want some dip?" I shoved the plate toward him.

He held out his hand. "Come on."

Well, why not? If I kept eating Fritos, my hips would be four inches wider by morning. As he put his arms around me, I saw the girls on the sofa staring at us and whispering. I didn't like the look on Mona's face. It's not a good idea to be on her hate list. Don't get steamed at *me*, Mona. This wasn't my idea.

"You have on a very nice dress tonight, Jeffi. You look good in blue."

At last someone noticed, even if it was Kurt. "Thanks."

He was an excellent dancer. I didn't have to concentrate on my feet the way I did with Paul Lambert. Kurt carried us both along. And he didn't suffocate me like Leon "Mohair" Bolonna. He knew exactly what he was doing. Except for Mona's eyes shooting daggers at me every time I faced her, I really didn't mind dancing with Kurt.

"Thank you," I said as the song ended. I started back to my Fritos.

"Wait," said Kurt, placing his hand on my shoulder. "They're putting on a new record."

I could feel Mona's knives in my back. "I thought maybe you'd want to dance with someone else now."

"No, I want to dance with you, Jeffi." He took my hand as the music started again.

This time, he talked while we danced. Most of the guys I've been with can't even chew gum while they dance. Not that we discussed anything deep. Just things like what we got for Christmas, how Steinbeck's *East of Eden* was going to be on TV again, and that we both wanted to be lawyers. Not once did Kurt bring up the history project or anything else about school. Maybe he had some positive points after all.

I never made it back to the Fritos. Kurt and I danced until Sara's father came. While she said good-bye to Pete, I headed up to Mona's bedroom for our coats. Mona was waiting at the front door when

I came down.

"What do you think you're doing, Jeffi Anders?" she snarled in a low voice. "I thought you liked Mike Hauser. Keep your mitts off Kurt."

"I'm not interested in getting my mitts on Kurt, Mona."

"Don't give me that. I saw how you were dancing together. Just because you can't get Mike doesn't give you the right to go after Kurt."

"I'm not planning on it."

Mona opened her mouth to say something, but at that moment Sara came up from the basement. "Thanks for inviting me, Mona." She took her coat from my hand. "It was a fabulous party."

Mona put on a perfect hostess smile and opened the door for us. I could feel the daggers all the way to the car.

"You and Kurt looked as if you were getting along really well tonight," Sara said, as her father drove toward my house.

"It was all right, I guess. Better than dancing with Butch."

"Kurt had his eyes closed while you were slow dancing. I was watching."

He did? "He was probably tired. Taking a cat nap."

"Jeffi, you're absolutely hopeless! Why do you insist on fighting your emotions?"

"What do you mean by that?"

"Forget it." Sara shook her head.

I turned away and looked out the car window. Big snowflakes floated onto the windshield. The sky had been clear before the party. Now the stars were gone, covered by clouds. I hate unexpected weather changes.

Did he really close his eyes?

8

The woolly-bear caterpillars were right about winter. As soon as we shoveled out from one storm, it started snowing again. The snow piles along the streets and sidewalks grew into small mountains. Whenever I left the house, I felt like a mouse wandering through a white maze.

If we hadn't had so much snow, nothing would have happened to Gram. I guess it *was* my fault, but I was tired of shoveling. Who could blame me for wanting a day off? I'd have scraped the back steps eventually, and Gram could have waited to fill her bird feeder. The finches wouldn't starve.

I knew something was wrong as soon as I saw Mom's car in the driveway when I came home from school. She never left work before 5:00 and it was only 3:30. Another car, which I didn't recognize, was parked out front.

"Gram's had an accident," Mom said as I burst through the door. She paced up and down the floor, frantic with worry. "Dr. Byrd is upstairs with her now."

"What happened? How . . . how bad is it?"

"That woman should know enough to stay off icy steps." Mom's voice rose in frustration. "A fall at her age! How could she be so foolish?"

Dr. Byrd came down the stairs carrying his black bag. He was probably the last doctor in the state who made house calls. I think he did it for us because Gram had known him since they were in grade school. He sat on the bottom step and reached for his rubber boots. "Hiya, Jeffi. My, you've grown into quite a young lady."

"How badly did she hurt herself?" Mom asked as she approached him anxiously. Her hands shook.

"Relax, Margaret. Nothing's broken. She'll be fine with a bit of rest." He pulled on his coat. "She has some bruises and torn ligaments around the knee. She should keep off her feet as much as possible for a few weeks. No stairs." As he opened the front door, a gush of frigid air blew in. "I gave her pills for the pain. She'll feel much better in a couple of days. I'll be back in a week or so to check on her."

That night, Ralph moved Gram's bed into the sewing room next to the kitchen. Then he carried her downstairs. I knew she was in pain because she didn't bother yelling about the scrapes he made on the wallpaper when he brought down the headboard.

Mom made a tuna casserole for dinner. It was awful. Since she hadn't cooked a meal since we moved in with Gram, you couldn't blame her. None of us ate much.

After Ralph and I cleaned up the dishes, I crept into the sewing room. Gram looked white and frail lying on her pillow. I never thought of her as old before that moment. "I'm sorry about your fall, Gram," I whispered.

She turned her head toward me. "Now don't you worry about this, Jennifer. It's nothing," she said weakly.

Carefully, I sat on her bed. "Who will take care of you when everyone is gone during the day?"

"I'm not an invalid. I can get up for the bathroom or to get something out of the refrigerator if I have to. But I won't be able to clean the house and cook like I used to."

"Oh," I said softly. For some reason it didn't seem right to speak at a normal volume.

"Jennifer, I'm depending on you to keep this household going."

"Me?"

"Neither Ralph nor your mother are very good at domestic chores."

"But, Gram, neither am I! Maybe we should hire a maid."

She pushed herself up on her elbows. "No stranger is going to touch my house. Especially when we can manage ourselves."

I knew then that the next few weeks would be harder on us than on Gram.

The next morning, I opened my eyes to see Sara standing over me. "I didn't think I'd ever get you awake." She pulled off the covers. "Hurry up. It's past eight already."

"Good grief! Why didn't Gram wake me? I'll never make it." Then I remembered that I couldn't depend on Gram's radiator-pipe signal any more.

I managed to slip into homeroom before the final bell, but my body was a disaster. I was stuck wearing my glasses since I hadn't had time to insert my contact lenses. My hair was pulled back in an ugly, rush-job ponytail, and I wore the same clothes I had worn the day before, because in my haste I'd grabbed the first thing I saw lying on my chair. By second period, my stomach growled like an angry grizzly because I'd missed breakfast. Worst of all, my teeth were covered with morning-mouth fuzz. My misery was lessened only slightly by Sara's giving me a stick of gum and Bethany's lending me money for lunch.

When I got home from school, Gram was asleep. Ralph's portable TV, on the table near the foot of her bed, droned on with an afternoon game show. I went into the kitchen for a snack. The place was a mess! The table was covered with bread crumbs and jelly. Dirty dishes, including a granola-caked cereal bowl and egg-smeared plate, were scattered over the counter. The kitchen smelled of coffee grounds and grapefruit rinds left in the sink. Gram must not have come in there all day. The way she feels about her kitchen, she would have cleaned it up, bad knee or not. I took an apple out of the refrigerator and went up to my room. No way was I going to clean up after Mom and Ralph.

Ralph brought home Chinese food for dinner and Mom cleaned

up the kitchen. When the evening news was over, Mom called a family meeting. "We all have to pitch in while Gram's laid up," she began.

"I didn't leave the kitchen looking like the back of a garbage truck," I said.

"I think we should hire a maid," said Ralph. "I don't have time to do housework and keep my practice going too."

"Gram won't put up with that. She already told me." I should have kept my big mouth shut.

Mom chewed her fingernail. If Gram didn't recover soon, Mom's hands would look like an absolute disaster. "I can do the shopping from Gram's list every week," she said. "Jeffi, you can start dinner when you get home and do any other chores Gram gives you. Ralph and I will do kitchen cleanup. Later we'll decide how to divide laundry and housecleaning."

"What about when I have band?"

"Ralph can bring home dinner on those days."

"But, Mom, I'm going to get stuck doing everything, I know it," I moaned.

"You have the most free time of the three of us, Jennifer. Anyway, it's only for a few weeks."

I knew I wasn't going to like this. If only I'd scraped the ice off the back steps.

For the first time in six years, I got up when my alarm went off. By the time I made it downstairs, Mom had gone to work. Ralph hid behind the newspaper drinking his coffee. "Better read the note Mom left you," he said as I poured some orange juice. "And you're supposed to ask Gram about dinner tonight."

"Did you eat yet?"

"Just toast. Mom made Gram's breakfast."

I popped a muffin into the toaster oven and checked the refrigerator for lunch. "There's nothing for sandwiches, Ralph. What are we supposed to do now?"

He put down his paper. "How about peanut butter? I'll make it while you see Gram." Yuk! I hated peanut butter almost as much as liverwurst.

By the time Gram had told me about thawing the meat, filling her bird feeder, putting out the empty egg cartons for the egg man, and presoaking Ralph's white shirts, Sara had arrived.

"Go without me," I told her as I stood at the front door with my arms full of shirts. "I have to get this stuff done before I leave."

"Are you going to be this late every morning?" she asked.

"We'll be back to normal tomorrow."

But the next day wasn't any better. In fact, Ralph had to drive me to school every day that week. After a couple of weeks we were more organized, and I started walking to school with Sara again. Yet even after I adjusted to the new routine, I felt as if I were running in high gear.

As soon as the three-o'clock bell rang each day, I rushed home to start dinner and do chores. Gram always had something that had to be done IMMEDIATELY. Not after Ralph and Mom came home. Not on the weekend. But THAT VERY MOMENT. I had to cut out my nightly calls to Bethany and Sara in order to have time for my homework. And I rarely watched television any more.

Mom and Ralph had problems too. Mom did the grocery shopping every Friday on her way home from work, so we knew she'd be at least two hours late. When she arrived, Gram would limp into the kitchen and watch her empty the bags. "You bought the wrong size again, Margaret," she'd say. "And you forgot the stuffing mix." Then Mom would take two aspirin from the bottle by the sink and go upstairs to lie down.

Ralph was in charge of cleaning. He looked ridiculous pushing around the vacuum and sticking his hand in the toilet bowl. I didn't tease him though, since he hadn't made a single wisecrack about my cooking—even the night the meat loaf crumbled and the baked potatoes exploded in the oven.

I think all three of us were counting the days until Gram was back to normal.

"Are you listening, Jeffi?" Bethany poked me with her pen as we sat in the back of Miss Longren's study hall.

"I'm trying to finish reading the English assignment. I didn't have time last night. Gram's driving me crazy with all her 'emergency' jobs."

"It can't be that much work." Sara turned around and leaned on my desk.

"It is!" I pushed her arm off my book.

"I hate to say it, Jeffi, but I think your grandmother had you spoiled. My mother would never let us get away with . . ."

"She doesn't need to hear that now, Sara," Bethany said sharply. "Anyway, I want to tell Jeffi about Frank and me — we're doubling with his 18-year-old cousin. We're going to the city to see the new Travolta movie. I don't have to be home until 1:00 A.M."

I tried to block her out and concentrate on *The Merchant of Venice*.

Bethany poked me again. "She's got it in for you, Jeffi."

"Who does?" I asked without looking up from my book.

"Mona. How I wish I'd been at that party to see her squirm!"

"She's not still mad about that? It was weeks ago."

Sara put her finger to her lips. "Not so loud, you guys. LuAnn's listening." LuAnn turned around and glared at us. Mona would be proud of her.

"Haven't you noticed how Mona gives you dirty looks all the time?" Bethany continued.

"I've noticed. But I'm not going to pay attention to her wild imagination."

Bethany raised her eyebrows. "From what I hear, she isn't imagining it."

"What did you hear?"

"Oh, nothing." The bell rang and Bethany picked up her books. "Have to meet Frank before history. See ya' later."

Sara and I walked into the hall. "Darn, I didn't finish my English. Next time, I'll go to the library."

"Bethany can get carried away," agreed Sara. "Are you going to the honor society meeting after school?"

"I forgot all about it."

"You'd better come. It's about the trip to Washington. All the new members will be there. I can't wait to see who was invited to join this year."

"I'll have to call Gram."

"I wish Pete had made it. I'd love to see the cherry blossoms with him. But he gets such awful grades in biology."

"So give him some private help," I teased, nudging her with my elbow. "Have you told Bethany about his being your Special Someone?"

"Not yet. But I will. Soon."

"Why do you keep hiding it? She's sure to notice one of these days if she ever stops swooning over Hook-shot. After Mona's party, it's certainly no secret to the rest of the school."

"I know. It's just . . . well, Bethany wouldn't understand why I like Pete. You know what she thinks of anyone who isn't tall, handsome, and athletic."

"Why should you care what she thinks?"

"Don't you ever worry about what people think?"

"Of course not." I flipped through my notebook so she couldn't see my face. I didn't want Sara to know I was lying.

Mr. Roscher stood at the door when Sara and I arrived in the guidance office after school. Most of the upperclassmen were already there. So were some new faces, including Kurt's. Mona sat next to him flirting as if there were no tomorrow.

"She has him cornered again," whispered Sara as we sat on the floor.

"Yeah, I noticed." I tried to sound as if I didn't care, but I did.

Mr. Roscher closed the door and began the meeting. "We will initiate 8 freshmen and 15 upperclassmen this year," he said. "The initiation ceremony will be February 26. Your parents are invited, of course." Mr. Roscher spent the next 20 minutes explaining the initiation exercises. He could have given us all the information in

5 minutes. Didn't he realize some of us had to get home?

"On the second Saturday in April," he continued, "our group will visit Washington. We will leave early in the morning and return that night by bus. If you went to New York last year, you know the honor society has a fund raiser to pay for the spring trip. At our next meeting, I want suggestions for money-raising activities."

"I hope we don't have to sell candy or greeting cards again," I said to Sara when the meeting ended.

"I hope not either," she moaned. "I'm sick of bugging my neighbors every time we have one of these trips. Maybe someone will think of a new idea."

I didn't get home until 4:15. Dinner would be late unless Gram knew a quick recipe. "Is that you, Jennifer?" she called as I closed the front door. "How was your meeting?"

"Fine." I walked into her room. "What do I do about dinner?"

"Bring me my cookbook and I'll pick out a casserole. You can put it together before your mother and brother get home." I started to leave. "Jennifer dear, have you watered my plants today? They need fertilizer, too, remember?"

"Yes, Gram. I'll do it."

"And, Jennifer, could you turn on "Donahue" for me?"

"What channel?"

"Three. You should hear the things he has on his show. Yesterday was about teen-agers. I never realized what went on in the schools these days. Shocking! I hope Daniel Boone isn't like that."

"It's not." I turned the channel.

"One other thing . . ."

"Yes, Gram." Not more!

"Could you bring a roll of toilet paper down from the upstairs bathroom?"

"OK."

"And empty the wastebasket."

I picked up the wastebasket. "Is your knee feeling any better?"

"Oh, it's getting more limber every day."

"I'm glad."

The last time I had talked to Mike was at the wrestling match. Since then, whenever I saw him, he was with Dyan or Patricia or one of the cheerleaders. Still, he waved when we passed in the hall. At least he knew I was alive. Bethany kept telling me he was worth the wait, but I figured my last chance with Mike Hauser had been snowed under by the blizzard. That's why I almost died of shock when he called Wednesday after dinner.

"We had a deal about plowing through algebra together, didn't we?" he said. I heard music playing in the background.

"Yes, I guess we did."

"I'm ready when you are."

I held the receiver tightly. "How about during study hall? We have one the same period."

"No, that wouldn't be enough time. I had in mind after school. Maybe a few times a week."

A few times a week! Mike Hauser wanted to be alone with me a few times a week! Bethany had been right again. I'd given up too soon. Then I remembered Gram's leg and getting dinner. "I don't know if I can stay late more than once a week."

"Well, if you can't, that'll have to do." He sounded as disappointed as I was. "I'll meet you tomorrow at your locker."

Ralph didn't mind when I asked him if he'd bring home dinner on Thursdays too. "Why not? You've been working hard around here lately," he said. "I might even throw a pizza together for us if I can get home early enough."

I wasn't sure if he were relieved to miss a night of my cooking or if he were being a nice guy. Things had changed at our house. A few weeks ago, Ralph would have hit the ceiling if I'd asked him for a favor.

The next afternoon, Mike and I found an empty classroom where we could study. I expected him to joke around for awhile, but instead, he had us working on algebra problems from the minute we sat down until his bus came an hour later. It wasn't exactly the romantic afternoon I'd dreamed about.

When I arrived home, I gave Bethany an urgent phone call. "All he wanted to do was study. What am I doing wrong?"

"You have to play this carefully," she said. "You can't let him get away now. Maybe he was shy. He needs you to break the ice."

"Mike Hauser, shy?" I asked incredulously.

"Sure. All guys are shy when they're alone with a girl they really like." How did she know so much about boys?

"How do I break the ice? It's hard to talk to him."

"Start with a subject he really likes. Then keep things rolling by asking him questions, pretending you need more explanation, flattering him. That's how you keep a guy hooked. Make him think you're interested in what he is."

"Do you mean you and Frank talk about *him* all the time?"

"Of course."

"Don't you talk about what you're interested in at all?"

"Listen, Jeffi," she said impatiently, "do you want Mike to like you or not?"

You can't quarrel with success and Bethany was undeniably a success with boys. I had a lot to learn. "I'll give it a try."

"Believe me, it can't fail."

Mike and I agreed to meet the following Thursday. Gram was peeved when I told her I'd be late again. She didn't mind if Ralph made dinner, but she was upset that I wouldn't be home to change the sheets that afternoon. I finally convinced her that it was a waste of time to tear the beds apart once they were already made and that I'd get up early the next morning and do it after everyone was out of bed.

In the beginning, it looked as if our afternoon together were going to be the same as before. The minute we sat down at the table in the conference room, Mike opened his book and began working. Our conversation was limited to variables and factoring, and the most romantic thing he said was "How do you do this problem?" It wasn't until we'd finished the last exercise that the ice cracked.

"Do you have time to go up to The Alley for a soda?" Mike asked as we gathered our books.

"I thought you had to catch the bus at four."

"Not today. My mother is picking me up after work." He helped me on with my coat. "How about it? My treat."

It wouldn't matter if I got home a little late. Besides, if I said no, he might never ask again. "Sure. I'd like that." Did this qualify as my first real date? It wasn't after dark, but Mike *had* asked me. And he *was* paying.

We slid into one of the back booths. I remembered Bethany's advice: start with a subject he enjoys. "How's your weight-lifting program coming?" I asked after we'd ordered.

"I've increased my biceps a half-inch already. And I can bench press 120 pounds."

Ask for more explanation. "Do you run too?"

"Yeah. A couple of miles every morning and 10 on weekends."

Flatter him. "No wonder you're in fantastic condition."

It was working. I had his attention. Mike Hauser was looking right at *me*, Jennifer Anders. Smiling at me with that incredibly handsome face. I'd finally mastered the technique.

"I talked my dad into buying me a weight set and a boxing bag. Now I work out in our basement." He cracked his knuckles as the waiter set our drinks and a plate of fries on the table.

Someone put a quarter into the jukebox. "I just bought that album. Do you like it?" I raised my voice so he could hear me over the music.

"One of the coach's friends couldn't believe I was only 16." Mike continued, ignoring my comment. "He said I had the muscles of a 19-year-old."

"Amazing."

The weight-lifting discussion went on for 20 minutes. I began to tire of nodding my head and saying, "That's great!" I couldn't think of any more questions to ask. When Mike stopped to eat the fries, I decided to make a final attempt at changing the subject.

"Bethany and Frank saw the new Travolta movie. They loved it."

He washed down his fries with a gulp of soda. "No kidding? Well, it'll probably be on the tube in a year. I'll wait to see it then."

"What kind of movies do you like?"

"My all-time favorite was *Rocky*. The fight scene was tremendous! I could feel the punches land. I can really identify with getting hit—some of the tackles I've had."

No matter what subject I tried—TV, classes, summer vacation—Mike turned the conversation to sports. I didn't know how long I could pretend to be interested. How do girls keep this up for an entire evening?

I was relieved when Tony Mantione came over to our table to mooch some fries. "I should go soon," I said as Tony made himself at home in our booth. "It's almost five."

"I'll walk you to the corner." Mike paid the bill and we left Tony with the rest of the French fries.

"Thanks for the soda," I said when we arrived at the corner.

"Hey, I enjoyed it. Same time next Thursday for more algebra antics?" He smiled.

"Sure."

When I reached the other side of the street, I turned to signal a final good-bye. But Mike had already started toward the school. I waved at his back.

What had gone wrong? My first date with the neatest guy in school and I was almost glad when it was time to go home. Dating was supposed to be more fun than this. I thought I'd followed all of Bethany's advice. Where had I made my mistake?

9

Bethany's phone was busy all night. Just my luck—the one time I desperately needed her advice. When I arrived in school the next morning, she was huddled in a corner of the lobby with Frank. I *had* to find out where I'd made my mistake with Mike. After the current-events quiz in first period history, I started a note to her. I didn't get far.

"I decided to have a class discussion today instead of my usual Friday lecture." Ms. Morgan leaned against the front of her desk.

Her announcement was met with mixed reviews, from moans to cheers. I was with the moaners. Now there was no way I could write a note to Bethany without being obvious.

"As you may know, smoking by students currently is prohibited anywhere on high school property. At issue is whether or not students should have a smoking lounge set aside for them. If this were approved by the administration, smoking by students would be allowed only in this lounge. Does anyone have an opinion?"

A few kids raised their hands. Most of the comments were pretty silly, like "Good idea if we can smoke anything we want," or "Will we have a cigarette machine too?" It looked as if the discussion would be a big failure. Maybe Ms. Morgan would give up and I could write the note.

Then she called on Kurt. "I think it's a good idea to set up a smoking lounge," he said. "Students who smoke will do it anyway. I'd rather have them doing it somewhere besides the bathrooms. Why should the rest of us have to breathe their smoke?"

Some others agreed with him. I could feel myself being pulled into the discussion. I couldn't let Kurt do it again. Now I *had* to voice my opinion. "Just because kids are breaking the rules isn't a good reason to set up a smoking lounge. If the school has a rule against smoking, it should enforce it."

Kurt raised his hand again. "The rule is unenforceable anyway. Teachers have to spend all their time between classes monitoring the bathrooms and outside doors. And they can't possibly catch everybody. Having a smoking lounge is better than having kids sneak outside."

The next thing I knew, Kurt and I were the only ones talking. Before long, we each had a cheering section.

"The school shouldn't condone smoking," I said, "while at the same time teaching us about the health hazards of cigarettes."

"But if teachers are allowed to smoke, so should students."

"I don't think teachers should be permitted to smoke in school either. Many public places forbid smoking. Teachers should set a good example."

"True. But what kind of example is it when a teacher refrains from smoking in school and lights up the minute he or she gets out the door at the end of the day? I say if people, students or teachers, want to smoke, let them do it where it won't bother others."

"And I say it's wrong for the school to encourage smoking by providing students with a smoking lounge. It's not even legal for minors to buy cigarettes. The school would be saying it's OK for kids to break the law."

If the bell hadn't sounded, Kurt and I probably would have continued our debate another half-hour. I hadn't had such an invigorating argument with anyone in a long, long time. It had been fun.

"No hard feelings, Jeffi?" Kurt asked as we left the room.

I shook my head. "Of course not. It was just a debate. I love arguing."

"I could tell!" He laughed. "You had a few good points, but I still don't agree with you."

"Then we're even. You didn't convince me either."

Taking a step closer, he cleared his voice. "Uh, I was wondering if you weren't doing anything . . ."

"What?" I asked expectantly. It almost sounded as if he were trying to ask me out.

"Oh, uh, guess I'll see you next period," Kurt said, looking behind me. His friendly smile faded.

I spun around. There stood Mike. "What's your next class?" He draped his arm around my shoulders. I should have felt a tingle of excitement when he touched me. Instead I felt uncomfortable.

"Biology," I replied.

"I'll walk you there." His arm stood still in place, he steered me down the hall. I turned my head to say good-bye to Kurt, but he was gone. I wished Mike hadn't appeared when he did. I wondered what Kurt had been going to say.

"What were you talking to him about?" Mike asked. For a second I thought he sounded jealous. No chance. Not THE Mike Hauser.

"We had a terrific debate in history class about the smoking lounge."

"Oh, yeah? Which side were you on?"

"I was against it."

"You're joking?" He laughed. "How could anyone be against it?" He seemed amazed that I could disagree with him.

"Why do you think there should be one?"

"Well, I don't know. It seems like a good idea. The teachers have a lounge. Students should too. We need a place to relax."

"But, Mike, the issue isn't whether the kids should have a lounge. It's whether smoking should be allowed there."

He shrugged. "Why waste time talking about it? We don't have a say one way or the other."

Didn't he understand that discussing issues can be just for fun?

"Can we get together twice next week?" he said, as we stopped outside the biology room. "I found out I'm having a huge algebra test next Friday."

"I think I can make it."

"We can stop at The Alley afterward. I'd really like to spend more time with you." He drew me closer.

Maybe I hadn't made any mistakes yesterday after all.

When I got home that afternoon, Gram had the cards set up on the kitchen table for whist. "I thought we'd play a few games before we started dinner," she said as I took off my coat.

"What do you mean, before *we* start dinner?"

"I can manage the salad and potatoes if you'll do the leg work and bring them to the table for me."

I hate whist, but if Gram were going to help with dinner for the first time in weeks, I figured I could endure a game or two. In the middle of the second game, there was a knock on the back door. The last person I expected to see when I opened it was Old Man Harvey.

"Have something for your grandmother," he mumbled, patting the lump under his ragged, gray coat.

"Who is it?" Gram called from the kitchen. "Invite the person in, Jennifer."

"Come in, Mr. Harvey." I opened the door wider.

Gram looked pleased to see him. "Sit down, Mr. Harvey." She motioned toward Ralph's chair.

"Brought these for you," he grunted as he pulled out a beautiful bouquet of red and yellow tulips from under his coat.

"Oh! They're wonderful, Mr. Harvey. You know how I love flowers after a long winter. Where did you ever find them in February?"

"Forced the bulbs." A hint of a smile flickered across his face.

"Honestly. You must have a green thumb! Get a vase, Jennifer. We'll put them right here on the kitchen table." Gram handed me the flowers. "Makes my day, Mr. Harvey. How very thoughtful!"

"How is the knee, Mrs. Bamburg?" he asked, as I ran water into the vase.

"Almost back to normal," Gram replied. "I can move around much more this week. Care for some tea, Mr. Harvey?"

"If it's no trouble."

"Jennifer, bring some tea for us, dear, would you?"

"Thank you, Mrs. Bamburg." He slipped off his coat.

Gram put her arm around my waist when I brought over the cups. "Jennifer has been such a help, Mr. Harvey. If it hadn't been for her, this house would be a shambles. I'm very proud of my granddaughter."

Nodding, Old Man Harvey looked at me with his piercing gray eyes. "You're a lucky woman, Mrs. Bamburg."

Hearing Gram say that made me feel good inside. "Gram, why don't you and Mr. Harvey visit awhile. I can get dinner by myself."

"Mr. Harvey, would you like to play whist?"

"Yes, Mrs. Bamburg, I would."

They played cards for over an hour until Ralph came home. Gram invited Old Man Harvey to stay for dinner, but he declined. "Gram, I said after he left, "I can't believe Mr. Harvey brought you flowers. He always acts as if he hates everyone."

"Just goes to show, Jennifer, that you can be wrong about people if you don't look deep enough."

I sure was wrong about Old Man Harvey.

It was a day worth celebrating when Dr. Byrd stopped by to check Gram's knee. "She won't be running the Boston Marathon this year," he told us, "but otherwise the old girl is back in A-1 shape."

That night, Gram made a scrumptious rib roast, golden potatoes, her special green-bean surprise, and a devil's-food cake covered with an inch of chocolate frosting. We all ate as if we hadn't had a decent meal in weeks.

It felt great to have the house back to normal. Gram didn't whiz around the way she had before the fall, but she still accomplished in one day what Ralph, Mom, and I needed a week to do. She took more rests on the recliner than she used to, and sometimes she'd ask me to finish a job she had started earlier in the day. I didn't mind helping now that I knew how much work it was to run a house. Besides, after six weeks I was used to it. I even woke up in the morning without Gram's signal.

With my afternoons free again, Mike and I studied together two or three days a week. The word got out about us, and his friends began saying hello to me in the halls. Even Dyan and Patricia spoke to me when I saw them in the girls' room.

But our relationship wasn't as romantic as people thought. In fact, we spent most of our time at the conference table discussing algebra. Mike took me to The Alley twice, but both times we shared a booth with his football buddies. Not exactly an intimate situation. I didn't mind though. Being with him was what mattered. Bethany said I must be doing something right because Mike continued to make study dates. "Be patient," she said. "You can't rush love."

So I was patient.

There was one other important thing I finally had time to do now that Gram was recovered: practice my clarinet. Ever since December, I'd planned to challenge Norma. This time I would be prepared. The Spring Concert was in a few weeks, and I wanted to be sitting in the first chair for it.

One day, Mr. Bonner announced that all challenges before the Spring Concert had to be held by mid-March, especially when a first chair was involved. "There are several solos in the concert music," he said, "and I want ample time to work with the soloists. For this reason, there will be no changes in seating after next Friday."

I challenged Norma that afternoon. I wasn't certain I could be ready by the following Friday, but it was my last chance. During the next week, I practiced every free moment. I played each scale over and over until I could finger faster and more accurately than I ever had before. I asked Mr. Bonner for new music in order to practice sight-reading. I played my clarinet so much I developed deep teeth marks on the inside of my lower lip and a hard callus on the side of my right thumb.

The day of the challenge finally arrived—Friday the 13th. I tried not to let the date bother me. It couldn't be bad luck for both of us. Norma would be a formidable opponent, but I'd done all I could to prepare. If she beat me again, it was because she was a better musician than I.

I went first this time. Mr. Bonner asked me to play three scales. I concentrated on accuracy and let the speed take care of itself. No mistakes! Sight-reading was more difficult. The music was full of trills and runs, which I fumbled slightly. I did better following key signatures and observing dynamic markings. It seemed an eternity until I reached the bottom of the page.

From my chair in Mr. Bonner's office, Norma's tryout sounded even better than in December. She had a different piece to sight-read, so I couldn't tell how she did on that, but her scales were clean. When she finished, Mr. Bonner called me out.

"Girls," he said tapping his baton on the music stand, "this isn't an easy decision. You both played extremely well." Norma nervously pushed her A-flat key up and down. "But keeping in mind that the winner will have a solo in the Spring Concert, I chose the person who played the sight-reading piece with the most expression."

My heart pounded like a tympany.

"Norma, you have fine technique," he continued, "and are one of the best clarinetists I've worked with here." She looked up from her lap and smiled shyly. "But Jeffi demonstrated that she has something extra: the ability to inject emotion into the notes. She made the music come alive. For this reason, I've awarded her first chair and the solo."

I didn't know whether to sigh with relief or run down the hall whooping with joy.

"Jeffi," Norma said as we put our clarinets away, "you played better today than I've ever heard you."

"Thanks. You sounded good too. I don't know how he decided on me."

"You *should* be first chair. What he said about your playing with feeling is true. I've noticed it before."

"I was just lucky today . . ."

"Oh, no," she said. "I never expected to beat you in December. I know it was because you had a bad day. But it was fun being first chair for a couple of months anyway."

I felt ashamed of all the times I'd put her down, and how nasty I'd been when she beat me. I don't often flatter people because it seems so awkward when I say it, but this time the words popped out before I stopped to think about them. "You know, Norma, you're a pretty neat person."

Her face broke into a huge grin. I'm not sure which one of us was happier.

The honor society fund raiser had started in early March. Because I was busy practicing, I hadn't done much about it. With the challenge over, I had time to work on the project.

One of the juniors came up with the Rent-a-Kid idea. Everyone agreed it was better than selling peanut brittle or holding a dozen bake sales. Each of us was to hire himself out to do chores and odd jobs. Mr. Roscher put an advertisement in the *Weekly Reporter* encouraging people in town to call with jobs they needed done. You could line up your own jobs or take them from Mr. Roscher's list. We had about a month to accumulate money and each person was responsible for earning his or her own fare. If you didn't have enough in your Rent-a-Kid account by the day of the Washington trip, you or your parents had to contribute the difference.

On the Saturday morning after the challenge, I woke early to plot my strategy. Since it was a beautiful, cloudless day, I took my pen and pad out to the porch. Spring was in the air—the smell of moist soil, the chirping of chickadees as they flitted around the bird feeder, the warmth of the sun streaming through the still-naked branches.

I had finished making a list of four or five people who might have jobs available when I glanced toward Old Man Harvey's yard. Stooping over his front flower bed, he poked under the leaves with the end of a rake. *Why not?* I thought. *All he can do is say no.*

I crossed the street to his house. "Terrific day, isn't it?" I called cheerfully to him from the sidewalk.

Hesitantly he straightened up and looked in my direction. He wore the same gray pants and ragged coat. "Not bad," he grunted.

"Makes you think spring is almost here." I walked closer. "Look, your crocuses are blooming already." I pointed to the yellow and purple flowers pushing through the leaves.

"Have to get this mulch off before the daffodils come up."

"Do you need help?"

He squinted at me from behind those thick glasses. "Why do you want to help *me?*" he asked gruffly.

"It's a school project we have. The honor society is going to Washington and I have to earn money for the trip."

He rubbed the white stubble on his chin with his gnarled fingers. "Honor society, you say?"

"That's right. You can pay me whatever you think is fair."

"You'll do it exactly as I tell you?"

"Yes," I replied and within five minutes I was raking leaves off his garden. He stood next to me watching everything I did and barking his orders.

"Pull it away from those crocuses with your hands. Gently now . . . you missed a spot by the fence . . . you can't do a good job with the rake stuck full of leaves. Clean it off."

As the morning progressed, I realized there were hundreds of people who would be easier to work for than Old Man Harvey.

After the flower beds were cleared, he said he needed his roof gutters cleaned out. "I can't get up on a ladder any more." He rubbed the small of his back. "They're so clogged up, they don't do any good. If you want to earn some more . . . ."

So we brought his ladder up from the basement. For the next hour, I pulled wet leaves out of his gutters and dumped them in an old bucket. When I finished, he took out his wallet and handed me ten dollars. "That fair?"

I had no idea how much the job was worth. "Thank you, Mr. Harvey." I put the money in my pocket.

"Never had anybody offer to work for me before. Most kids are too lazy to do a decent job anyway." His face softened for a moment. "You did good work."

"Thanks." I smiled. "If you ever need help again, let me know. I can do housework too."

"I'll keep that in mind."

I headed home, ten dollars richer and three hours sorer. As I opened our front door, I looked back across the street. Mr. Harvey sat on his porch steps, the sunlight reflecting off his glasses. Slowly he raised his hand and waved.

I was doing my Spanish translations Sunday night when Ralph knocked on my door. "There's a guy on the phone. Don't tie up the line too long. I'm expecting a call."

"How goes it, Jeffi?" I heard Mike say when I picked up the receiver.

"I was just fooling around with my Spanish."

"Doesn't sound very exciting."

"It's not. Are you having trouble with the algebra homework or something?"

He laughed. "Algebra's the farthest thing from my mind. I called about a big party next Saturday night."

"Oh?" I held the phone tight against my ear so I wouldn't miss a single word.

"Patricia O'Reilly's having a party to celebrate St. Patrick's Day. It should be a real blast. Want to come?"

Don't let him know you've been waiting for this moment all year. I swallowed hard so my voice wouldn't quiver. "That would be fun. I'd like to go."

"Great." Mike didn't sound at all surprised that I accepted. "I'll pick you up around 7:30. I'll try to borrow my dad's car. Don't forget to wear green.''

We talked for another 20 minutes about the new video game his family had bought and about the boxing match he'd seen on television that afternoon. Finally I had to end the conversation when Ralph stood next to the phone pointing at his watch.

Patricia's party was the hot topic all week. For the first time, *I* was going to be part of a major Daniel Boone happening. I, Jeffi Anders, one-time wallflower, asked to a real party. Not some juvenile affair like Mona's, but a bona fide teen-age party, and by one of the most popular boys in school! A star football player, tall, dark, handsome who chose *me* over the hundred other girls who would give their favorite designer jeans to date him.

"I knew he'd ask you eventually!" squealed Bethany. "Didn't I tell you that the day you rode to school with him? Now that you're dating Mike, you'll be invited every time someone in that crowd has a party."

"What are you going to wear?" Sara asked.

"I don't know yet. Something green.''

"It should be a wild party,'' said Bethany.

"What do you mean?"

"You'll find out!" she said cryptically. "What did your mother say?"

"Nothing. She thought it was nice that Mike asked me."

I didn't want to tell them about Mom's questions. Would Patricia's parents be home? Was Mike a good driver? What other kids would be there?

I knew if I answered that I didn't know for sure, she'd make me ask Mike. Or worse, she'd call Patricia's mother. Nobody's parents acted like that any more. I hated lying to Mom, but I couldn't let her ruin everything, especially after I worked all year to get this far. My whole future was at stake. Besides they weren't exactly lies. They might even turn out to be true.

10

What if Mike puts the move on me? Will I know what to do? I've read all about romance, but reading about it isn't the same as having one. I've never even been kissed on the lips.

You can't fake it. Bethany's brother says guys can tell if you're inexperienced. Unless they're as inexperienced as you are. I bet Mike has had plenty of practice.

I wish I could talk to someone. Mom would flip if she knew I were even thinking about things like this. And I don't want Bethany and Sara to discover how out of it I really am.

The doorbell rang at 7:45. Though I'd been ready since 7:00, I stayed in my room. Bethany says if you wait at the front door, you look too eager. When I came down, Mike was in the living room. He looked fantastic in his beige cords and green flannel shirt. I almost pinched myself to be sure this wasn't a dream.

"We've already made introductions," Ralph said.

"Please sit down, Mike." Mom motioned to the chair by the fireplace.

"No, thank you, Mrs. Anders. We should be going. There's another couple waiting in the car."

"You could invite them in. I'd like to . . ."

"We really have to go, Mom," I said, putting on my coat. Gram frowned at me. I ignored her.

Mom followed us to the front door. "When will you be bringing Jennifer home?" she asked Mike.

"I'll have Jeffi home by 11:30 at the latest. I hope that's all right."

"As long as I know where she is." Mom smiled at Mike. I felt as if I were back in kindergarten.

"Yes, ma'am. It was a pleasure to meet all of you."

"I hope we see you again soon." Mom opened the door.

We got out of the house not a minute too soon. I was lucky none of them embarrassed me. I could imagine Gram saying, "Oh, Mike, let me take a snapshot of you and Jennifer. This is her VERY FIRST date, you know." Or Mom: "You'll have to excuse Jennifer while she washes off all that unnecessary eye make-up."

"You look great tonight," Mike said. "I like your hair that way. It looks so natural."

"Thanks." I was glad he noticed. I'd spent 30 minutes getting it to look that way.

"I couldn't get my own wheels tonight," Mike said as we approached the car. "We'll be chauffeur-driven instead. You don't mind, do you?"

"Uh, no. Why should I?" And Mom expected Mike to be driving. There was one lie I'd told.

He opened the back door of the car and I slid in. Three people sat in front. "You know Tony, don't you?" asked Mike. "This is his date, Lori. She goes to St. Pius. And Tony's brother, Johnny."

As soon as Mike closed the door, Johnny shifted into gear and pulled out. About ten yards down the street, he did a sharp U turn and sped past our house. I grapped the back of the front seat to steady myself.

"That was an S.O.B. turn, kids!" Johnny shouted over the roar of his broken muffler.

"A what?" Mike yelled.

"Slide Over, Baby! Worked, didn't it?" Johnny looked over his shoulder and laughed.

Why couldn't Johnny drive more carefully, at least until we were past my house? If Mom were watching, and I was sure she was, she'd be having a fit by now.

"This is going to be a real blowout party," Mike said as we turned onto Lewis Road. "I hope you drank lots of milk before you came."

"Why?"

"Haven't you heard of that trick? You can drink about twice as much that way. Coats your stomach."

"Oh, yeah, I knew that. I guess I forgot."

Tony turned around. "So much the better, eh, Mike?" They all laughed. I wasn't sure what the joke was, but I couldn't let them know. I joined in the laughter.

Mike leaned forward. "Hey, Johnny, I just remembered something I left at my place. Do you mind stopping for a second?"

"Come on," Tony moaned. "Can't it wait?"

"No way. It's part of my survival kit. It's on the way, so quit complaining."

In a few minutes, we skidded to a halt in front of Mike's house. Johnny left half his tire tread on the road. "What a car! Stops on a dime." He revved the motor. "Make it snappy, Hauser."

"Do you want to stay here or come in?" Mike asked as he opened the door. Without hesitating, I got out after him.

We entered the house through the back door. A dark-haired girl of about 17 sat at the kitchen table cutting out a sewing pattern. "Did Mom and Dad leave yet?" Mike asked her.

The girl looked up from her material with a bored expression. "Fifteen minutes ago."

"Good. Jeffi, this is Ivy, my sister. I'll be right down."

Ivy returned to her work. "Pretty material," I said, when I couldn't stand the silence any longer.

"What'd you say your name was?" she asked, putting down her scissors.

"Jeffi Anders."

"You must be the girl who's tutoring Mike."

"Tutoring?"

"In algebra, right?"

"Well, we study together sometimes, but . . ."

"I'm glad his taste in women is improving. I thought he didn't know any girls with IQs higher than their shoe size."

"Really?" I fumbled with the buttons on my coat.

"It's nice of you to save Mike's neck. My parents almost lynched him when his fall algebra grade came."

"What do you mean?"

"Didn't Mike tell you? If he doesn't bring up his grades, my parents won't let him play football next year. You should have seen the fur fly the night they told him. Wow!"

Why hadn't Mike ever mentioned getting low grades? And what did Ivy mean about tutoring?

"Whose fur is flying?" Mike bounced down the stairs. Under his arm was a grocery bag containing a box-shaped object.

"Forget it." Ivy started to cut her material again.

Without saying good-bye to her, Mike led me outside and closed the door.

"Mike, I want to talk to you about something Ivy said."

"Don't pay any attention to her," he said quickly. "She's one of those boring, intellectual grinds. She spends half her time worrying about getting into college and the other half huddled over a book. When you mention a party, she thinks you're talking politics. You know, Democrat or Republican."

"But I just wondered what she meant about . . ."

"We can talk about it later. Now I'm ready to party!" He pushed down on the front end of Johnny's car, causing it to rock wildly.

"Cool it, kid," Johnny yelled from inside, "or you can walk!"

Mike and I got into the front seat because Tony and Lori had transferred themselves to the back. "I had to send them where they'd have more room to maneuver," Johnny laughed hoarsely.

"Can't you wait until we get there, Lover Boy?" Mike teased.

Tony mumbled something out of the corner of his mouth, then returned to his clinch. How could they do that in front of us? Weren't they embarrassed? I sure was!

When we arrived at Patricia's, Mike didn't bother knocking. As he pushed the door open, loud music and smoky air greeted us. My skin tingled at the thought of entering the party with the best-looking guy in the place. Soon I forgot all about what Ivy had said.

The living room was jammed with kids dancing, lounging on the furniture, and standing around with cups in their hands. The only light in the room had a green bulb. If it hadn't been for the stream of light coming from the kitchen, I couldn't have made out anybody's face through the greenish haze. Mike took my hand and led me into the kitchen. It was as crowded as the living room.

"Hauser, old buddy!" Jake Moulton thumped Mike on the back. "Time to party! Let me get you some brew."

"I brought my own." Mike pulled a six-pack of beer from the paper bag under his arm.

"Save it. Patricia ordered a keg." Jake picked up two cups and filled them from the tap of a large metal container next to the kitchen door. He handed them to Mike.

So this was what Bethany meant about wild parties. Beer! I couldn't believe Patricia's parents let her serve it, not to mention buy a whole keg. Mom would have a cerebral hemorrhage if she knew I'd come within 20 feet of the stuff.

"Can you believe it? The stuff is green!" Mike exclaimed, holding out a cup to me.

"What do you expect? It's St. Patrick's Day," Patricia said as she entered the kitchen. She was gorgeous, as usual. Her green sweater and long, red hair made her look as if she belonged in an Irish travel commercial. She put her arm around Mike's shoulders and kissed his check. "Have a good time. You too, Jeffi. Let me know if you need anything." She refilled her cup with green beer and flitted back into the living room.

"Aren't you going to take it?" Mike thrust the cup toward me.

I stared at the tiny shamrocks printed on the plastic cup. Greenish foam lapped at the rim. "No, I don't think so."

"I don't blame you. The color makes me kind of sick, too. We can open my beer."

"Uh, do you think they have any soda?"

"That's a good one!" Mike laughed. He was laughing so hard he could barely get the words out. "Jake, can you make Jeffi a Shirley Temple cocktail?"

"I was only kidding," I said, trying to cover up my mistake. Hoping nobody saw how red my face was, I took the beer can from his hand. I swallowed a mouthful and almost gagged.

Mike pulled the tab off his can and grabbed my hand. "Let's go dance."

Soon there were more than 50 people in the house, many of them juniors and seniors. All of them were part of the "in" crowd. Someone pushed a few chairs into the hallway to make more room for dancing, and one of the guys turned up the stereo. At last, I realized that Mr. and Mrs. O'Reilly weren't home. That made another lie.

"Want another beer?" called Mike, over the music. I shook my head. He'd had four cans in the hour and a half we'd been there. I hadn't had anything since that first sip. My throat was parched from all the smoke and dancing. *A soda over crushed ice would taste heavenly*, I thought.

While I waited for Mike to return from the kitchen with his beer, Dyan Warren tapped my shoulder. "You look as if you're having a great time. But who wouldn't if she were with Mike."

"He's lots of fun." I said the words automatically. That was what I was supposed to say, wasn't it? Even if I weren't sure if I meant them any more.

"You're a lucky girl, Jeffi. I wish I were in your shoes."

Mike staggered across the floor toward us. Coating his stomach with milk hadn't done a very good job of keeping him sober. "Come on, Jeffi. They're having a drinking contest for couples." He slurred his words. "See who can chug the fastest."

"You should win that hands down," laughed Dyan.

"Let's hurry before they start." Mike tugged at my arm.

"I don't think I'd be such a good partner," I said hesitantly.

Mike looked crestfallen. "Don't back out on me. It has to be couples."

"I'll be your partner, Mike." Dyan slipped her arm through his. Her voice sounded silkier than usual. "That is, if Jeffi doesn't mind."

"Go ahead. I'll just watch."

The seven couples, including Mike and Dyan, stood around the keg in the kitchen. Patricia handed out cups. "The first pair to drink six cups apiece wins. And the guy can't help the girl by drinking some of hers."

As people pushed into the kitchen to watch, I found myself flattened against the refrigerator door. I could barely breathe. Everyone was clapping and cheering.

"Better catch Sandy," someone shouted as one of the girls passed out after her third cup. She looked as green as the beer. They all laughed.

"Hurry! Open the back door before she throws up in here."

"Let her through!" More laughter.

It didn't seem funny to me. In fact, I couldn't stand watching any more. I elbowed my way through the crowd and collapsed on the sofa in the empty living room. Is this what the "in" crowd thinks is so much fun: throwing up and passing out? Why would anyone *try* to act so stupid? My head pounded as if the entire percussion section were marching inside it. What was I doing here?

Finally the contest ended and the living room filled up again. Mike plopped down on the sofa next to me. "Some partner Dyan turned out to be. Gave up after only four." He belched.

His beer breath nauseated me. "Sorry you lost."

"Let's go upstairs," he murmured as he put his arms around me and squeezed. Too hard.

"What for?"

"We'll think of something," he said smirking.

Suddenly his hands were all over me as if he were an octopus attacking. I pushed him away. "I want to go home."

"Drink a little more. Then you'll feel like partying." He picked up my can from the end table. "It's full!" he bellowed. Everyone in the room looked at us.

"Please, let's go!"

"What's wrong with you?" He put his arms around me again. "Maybe if you lie down, you'll feel better."

"Take your hands off me!" I shouted as I shoved him and stood up.

"I knew I shouldn't have asked you to this party!" His face was red and ugly.

"Then why did you?"

He took a gulp from my can. "I wish I knew."

"It was so I'd keep tutoring you, wasn't it?"

"So what if it was?" He shrugged. I wanted to smash all his perfect white teeth.

"You used me, you creep!" I spun around. Tears pushed on the corners of my eyes. Don't cry. Not here. I rushed into the hall. A dozen kids were watching Jake and Tony do wobbly handstands. I nearly knocked Jake over as I ran by.

"Hey, look out!" someone yelled.

Grabbing my coat from the pile on the stairs, I flew out the door. I didn't stop running until the din from Patricia's house faded into the quiet of the night. But I could still feel Mike's hands pawing me, and smell the beer and smoke, and see them all laughing.

I'd walked a couple of miles along the dark road when I stopped thinking about the party long enough to realize I had to find a way home. I could hitchhike, but the road was lightly traveled. Besides, I didn't like the idea of getting into a strange car in the middle of the night. I tried to recall if we'd driven past a gas station or store or some place that had a phone booth. Then I remembered I didn't have any money. It was after ten. Mom would be playing bridge at the Simpsons'. What would she do if I called her? Probably blast me for lying and never let me go to another party for the rest of my life.

I saw the lights of a house a few hundred feet ahead. Something about the old yellow car sitting in the driveway was familiar. Where had I seen it before? That's it! It belonged to one of Gram's friends from Golden Age group.

A white-haired man, who looked like Santa Claus, answered

my knock. His wife sat on an overstuffed chair in the living room. She stood up when she saw me at the door.

"Well, if it isn't Lydia Bamburg's granddaughter. My goodness, what are you doing way out here, dear?"

"A little car trouble. Could I use your phone, please?"

She smiled sweetly and pointed to the phone. Thank goodness she didn't ask any more questions. I prayed Ralph would be home. Gram never drove at night and would only tell me to call Mom.

"Ralph?" I said when I heard his voice.

"Jeffi, are you all right? You sound upset."

"Can you come and get me?" I turned my back to the elderly couple and lowered my voice. "Please don't tell Gram or Mom."

There was a moment of silence.

"Please, Ralph . . ."

"OK. Where are you?"

I repeated Santa Claus's directions. "And hurry, Ralph."

When his car pulled into the driveway, a wave of relief swept over me. For the first time that night, I felt safe. "You didn't tell Gram, did you?" I asked, as I fastened my seat belt.

"She thinks I went out for pizza. If you're lucky, she'll be in bed when we get home."

I stared out the window at the bushes and trees passing by. They seemed to be laughing at me too.

"Want to talk about it?" Ralph said softly.

His voice broke the dam holding back my tears. "My whole life is ruined!" I sobbed. "I'll be a social reject for the rest of high school."

Ralph slowed down and steered onto the shoulder of the road. "Want to tell me what happened?" He turned off the ignition.

"I tried to do all the right things. I thought I'd finally made it too. Mike Hauser asked me to a party and all the most popular kids were there. Now I've made a mess of everything!"

Ralph took a tissue from the glove compartment and handed it to me.

"Wait until the word gets out about me Monday. They'll all

laugh. I'll never get asked out again." I crumpled the tissue in my fist.

"Tell me about this Mike Hauser."

"I thought he was *so* neat. But he's just a dumb, conceited jock. What did I ever see in him?" With my finger I drew a wavy line on the steamed-up windshield. "Ralph, he pretended to like me only so I'd tutor him in algebra." It hurt to admit it.

"Doesn't sound like a very nice guy."

The flood of tears started again. "They were drinking and . . . and, Ralph, I couldn't stand being there. Everyone says that's what high school's all about. And I hated it. What's wrong with me?"

"Not a thing, Jeffi." Ralph put his arm around me. I leaned against him. "Even though I haven't been in high school for a long time, I can guarantee you that all high school parties aren't like that, the same way all guys aren't like Mike. You have to find someone who makes you feel comfortable. You will, I'm sure."

"Who would ask me out after the way I acted? Everyone will think I'm a baby."

"It took maturity for you to leave that party. The easy thing would have been to go along with it. But standing up for your values takes real guts."

"I don't feel mature. I'll be 16 next month and I feel totally out of it."

"Listen, Jeffi, there's more to being mature than drinking beer and making out in dark corners. Believe me, I've had to go through it too."

"You always seem so secure and confident. I never thought you felt like this."

"Well, I did and still do sometimes." He chuckled. "Growing up is like climbing a ladder. You go up one rung at a time. The climb might be so easy you don't even realize you're doing it. Other times you think you'll never get any higher. And it can really hurt while you're climbing. But later, when you look back at how far you've come, you feel good."

"Do you think I climbed up a step tonight?"

"I think you climbed a few of them," he said, patting my shoulder.

"Thanks, Ralph."

"That's what big brothers are for. Now, what do you say we go get that pizza?"

I felt warm all the way to my toes. I reached across the seat and gave him a big hug.

11

On Monday morning, the entire school was buzzing about Patricia's party. At least my name wasn't in the headlines. Everyone was more interested in how Jake ordered two more kegs and what terrible hangovers the party-goers had Sunday.

When I passed Mike on the way to homeroom, he walked by me as though I weren't there. And guess what? I didn't mind the snub. The days when Mike Hauser could give me a fluttery heart were gone for good. If I felt anything, it was more like a sick stomach. If only I hadn't wasted most of the year chasing him!

But that chapter of my life wasn't quite over.

"This is the only place I can say what I have to without embarrassing you," said Bethany after she dragged me into the courtyard at lunch.

"You might be part polar bear, but I'm not ready to start eating outside yet," I said shivering.

Ignoring me, Bethany put her tray on a picnic table. She beckoned to Sara who stood at the cafeteria door.

"If this is about the party. . ."

"You're darn right it is. How could you be so uncouth? But then, maybe you don't care what people think of you any more." She looked at me scornfully.

"Dyan made a point of telling us how you ran out on Mike," said

Sara, as she sat down next to me.

"What got into you?" Bethany tapped her fork nervously. "Running home from a terrific party. Dumping a fantastic guy like Mike."

"For your information, fantastic Mike Hauser was using me to get free tutoring and I was too dumb to realize it. As for Patricia's parties, they're only terrific if you enjoy watching people make idiots of themselves."

Bethany's mouth dropped open. "How can you say that? Everyone knows they're THE Crowd."

"I don't care what everyone else thinks. I don't belong with people like Mike and Patricia."

"What am I supposed to say when someone asks me why you've turned into such a glop?"

"Bethany," I shot back, "if you're ashamed to have me as a friend, I'm sorry. But I know I don't want to be part of that crowd."

"Talk to her, Sara," Bethany fumed. "She'll listen to you. Tell her how foolish she's being."

Sara intently studied her tray.

"Sara?" Bethany repeated.

Sara looked straight at Bethany and pinched her lips together. "I think Jeffi's right. And I admire her for saying it."

"What?"

"If Mike used her that way, he *is* a jerk."

"But, Jeffi," Bethany said as she turned her back on Sara, "you finally made it into The Crowd and you're throwing it all away. You'll be left out of all the fun for the rest of high school."

"I'm not playing any more games. I wasn't very good at it in the first place. I'll take my chances being plain old Jeffi Anders."

Sara clapped. "If Jeffi can be honest, so can I. You want to know something, Beth? I'm crazy about Pete Symons—even if he doesn't have big muscles. And I'm sorry I didn't say so before."

Bethany looked dumbstruck. "What's wrong with you two? Don't you care about anything any more?" She snatched her tray and strode inside.

"Oh, no!" moaned Sara. She's taking this personally. She acts as if we deserted her."

"She'll get over it. I hope."

"I'm glad I told her about Pete. I feel as if a weight's been lifted off me."

"Yeah, I know exactly what you mean."

Bethany performed an expert job of avoiding Sara and me. When I called her the next day, she cut me off by saying she expected a call from Frank. Sara didn't have any luck either. Finally we decided to let her get over it in her own good time.

The gossip about Patricia's party died down within a few days. I put Mike and that whole horrible episode out of my mind and concentrated on schoolwork again.

Later that week, Mrs. Amadon announced a special contest in biology class. She explained that it would serve as a review for our unit exam on the human body. The class would be divided into two teams. Each person had to write ten questions, with answers, about the body. Mrs. Amadon would read the questions submitted by one team to a person on the other team. If you missed a question, you were out of the contest. It sounded like fun.

During the weekend, I pored over my notes, my textbook, the encyclopedia, and even one of Ralph's medical books, searching for the toughest questions I could find. By Sunday night, I was psyched for the contest. The next day, Mrs. Amadon assigned teams. I ended up on Team A. So did Bethany, although she made a point of standing as far away from me as she could.

Team B won the toss and Butch Norcross got the first question. "Remember, class, no one except Butch may answer. No coaching from teammates. You have 30 seconds, Butch. Good luck. What part of the brain controls balance?"

"Cerebellum," he said confidently. Butch is not known for his science sense; evidently he had studied hard for the contest.

"Right. Now a question for Team A. LuAnn, what is the medical name for the collarbone?"

LuAnn looked blank. I concentrated on the answer. Maybe she'd get it through telepathy.

"Clavicle," she said, just a second before her time was up. Right.

The questions gradually became more difficult. By the time it was my turn, five people on my team had missed. "Jeffi, how many bones are in the skull?"

This was one I remembered reading. Two ears, two eyes, two-two. "Twenty -two." Mona made a face. It must have been one she submitted.

By the final ten minutes of the period, only Cheryl Jones and I were left from Team A. Kurt, Sara, and Butch were still up for Team B. Then Cheryl and Sara missed. My turn again.

"In which organ is the semilunar valve found?"

"The heart." My team cheered.

"Butch, what is the medical name for the wrist bones?"

"Metacarpals," he answered quickly.

"I'm sorry," said Mrs. Amadon. "The matecarpals are the hand bones. Carpals are the wrist bones."

Butch muttered under his breath, then sat down.

Me again. "Which vitamin is necessary for blood clotting?"

"K."

"Way to go, Jeffi! Keep it up. You can beat them."

Mrs. Amadon turned to Kurt. "What are the smallest blood vessels called?" An easy one. I knew he'd get it.

"Capillaries."

As Team B applauded, the bell rang. "We'll finish tomorrow," called Mrs. Amadon as everyone charged for the door. "We'll play until either Jeffi or Kurt misses."

In English class next period, Sara turned around to talk before Miss Fuller arrived. "A head-to-head conflict! This is exciting! I'm glad it's Kurt you're up against. Otherwise, our team wouldn't have a prayer."

"You still don't," Pete said. "Jeffi's going to win for us, right, kid?"

"Right."

"You'd better win," Tommy Jagger called across the room. "I've got a five-dollar bet with Butch that you will. Don't let me down."

"I'll try not to."

Mona stopped at my desk on her way down the aisle. "Don't count on it," she sneered. "Kurt is going to study extra hard tonight. He told me himself. Besides he's smarter than you. He proved that today."

"What's that supposed to mean?" I asked.

"You had easier questions than Kurt."

"That's not true, Mona, and you know it!"

"What I *know* is that from the day Kurt came here, you stopped being Top Brain in the sophomore class."

Her comment stung. "Why don't you shut up?"

"Don't let her get to you, Jeffi," Pete whispered.

Mona sniffed and walked away.

"That girl really bugs me," Sara said.

"She's on *your* team."

"I don't care about that. It bothers me the way she's been putting you down ever since her party."

The bell rang and Miss Fuller started class. My mind kept drifting from infinitives and indirect objects to veins and ventricles. The team was counting on me. I had to beat Kurt. Not just for them, but for me.

The next morning during homeroom, a couple of girls from my team made signs for the Big Contest: "Win with Cranium Anders" and "Team A Accelerates to the Top." When we walked into biology third period, Team B had its own supply of "Go Kurt" signs. The room looked like a pep rally.

Then I saw a substitute at Mrs. Amadon's desk.

"We're going to finish the contest today, aren't we?" Butch called out.

The substitute, Mrs. Edwards, flipped through some papers. "Mrs. Amadon's note says the decision is up to the class. You can have a study hall or the contest."

"The contest!" everyone shouted. Kurt and I exchanged looks across the room. He smiled and mouthed, "Good luck." I wondered if he wanted to beat me as much as I did him.

Mrs. Edwards nodded. "I guess it's unanimous. I have all the questions right here. If someone will fill me in on the rules, we can begin." Mona jumped out of her chair and rambled off the procedure. I knew she couldn't wait to see me humiliated.

Kurt and I stood at the front of the room facing our teams. Each time Mrs. Edwards read a question, the room was absolutely quiet. When she said "correct," one of the teams would erupt into jubilant applause. With each question, more excitement filled the air.

Like the day before, the questions were easy in the beginning. About 15 minutes into the period, Kurt got the first hard one. "Which organ weighs six pounds and is the largest in the human body?"

Closing his eyes, Kurt rubbed his forehead. I was fairly sure I knew the answer, but just the same, I was glad it was his turn.

"Skin," he said. It was correct.

"What tissue joins bone to bone?"

I hesitated. Tendon or ligament? It was easy to confuse. Bone to bone. Like to like. L. "Ligament," I replied.

Mrs. Edwards glanced at her answer sheet. "That's right."

"Good job, Jeffi!" yelled Tommy.

"You can do it!"

"Kurt, how many alveoli are found in the average human lung — 3 million, 30 million, or 300 million?"

"Three hundred million."

If he hadn't answered so quickly, I'd have sworn it was a lucky guess.

We continued for another 20 minutes. The period was almost over, yet neither of us had missed a question. "We only have time for a few more," said Mrs. Edwards. "Kurt, to within the nearest five percent, what percent of bone is composed of water?"

For the first time, Kurt's self-assured expression faded.

'Come on, Kurt, you know it," Butch shouted.

"Shush," said Mona. "Let him think."

Kurt shifted from one foot to another and chewed on his lower lip.

"Five seconds."

"Twenty percent?" Kurt said hesitantly.

"No, I'm sorry. That's incorrect. The answer is 35 percent."

Team A went wild. Everyone cheered my name and waved signs. Even Bethany clapped. Tommy jumped across a chair toward Butch with an outstretched palm. "Pay up. I told you Jeffi would win."

But I knew I hadn't won. I remembered reading about the water content of bone in one of Mrs. Amadon's reference books. I was positive Kurt was right.

"Congratulations," Kurt said. Then, head down, he slowly walked back to his seat. Winning *had* been as important to him as it had to me.

He hadn't been sure of his answer. If I kept my mouth shut, no one would know the difference and I would win. But I knew Kurt was right, even if he had guessed. If I told Mrs. Edwards, my team would hate me. And what if I missed the next question?

I didn't want to beat Kurt this way.

"Mrs. Edwards," I said walking over to her desk.

"What?" She cupped her hand around her ear. "I can't hear you over the screaming."

"I think we should check that answer," I shouted.

Suddenly the classroom was silent. All eyes were fixed on me.

"The answer you have on the sheet is wrong. I can show you in the book over there. I'll get it."

"Jeffi, are you crazy?" shrieked Tommy. "We had them! What are you doing?"

"That was my question," Cheryl muttered. "Kurt was wrong."

I found the book and brought it to Mrs. Edwards. "Well," she said after she read the paragraph, "I'm afraid we goofed. The precise answer is 21 percent. Kurt was correct."

This time, Team B broke into applause. Butch yanked Kurt from his seat and pushed him up to the front again.

"We must hurry if we're going to break the tie." Mrs. Edwards paged through the sheet of questions. "I don't think Mrs. Amadon wants this to run into another day." She turned to me. "What is the yellowish pigment with chemical formula $C_{33}H_{36}O_6N_4$ that is an end product from the breakdown of hemoglobin?"

My mind went blank. I couldn't let myself look at my teammates. I knew they would be glaring at me. Don't get distracted. Think.

Yellow pigment. Hemoglobin. That's in red blood cells. It was coming to me. Yellow skin means jaundice. Because the liver doesn't work right. Liver. *Bile*. Red blood cells. *Ruby* red. "Bilirubin!"

Mrs. Edwards nodded. Kurt's team moaned, but my team was quiet. Then one voice called out, "Good job, Jeffi!" It was Bethany waving a sign. "Cheer for her, you turkeys!" One by one, the signs reappeared.

At that moment, the bell rang. The contest had ended in a tie. "I'll inform Mrs. Amadon of the results," said Mrs. Edwards, as we collected our books. "A tie should make both sides happy."

That's what she thought! A tie isn't as good as a win and everyone knew it. But I'd done the right thing even if some people didn't like it.

As I crossed Walnut Street on the way home that afternoon, I heard footsteps running behind me. I turned to see Kurt.

"Mind if I walk with you?" he asked, catching his breath.

"I thought you lived in the other direction."

"I do." His cheeks reddened. Was he blushing?

All those confusing feelings I'd had about Kurt started to make sense. I was glad he was there. "Sure, I'd like the company."

"Thanks for what you did today." He pushed a lock of blond hair off his forehead. "You knew I guessed when I said 20 percent, didn't you?"

"You gave the right answer. That's what counts."

"Your memory is incredible. If we'd gone longer, I would have lost for sure. I didn't know some of your questions near the end."

"Memory isn't everything. I wish I were as good as you in math.

You're probably the only student Trimble ever has liked."

"I suppose everyone's good at different things." He kicked a stone off the curb. "I'm awful at poetry."

He demonstrated with a feeble attempt at rhyme. "Roses are red, violets are blue. I wish I could write a good haiku."

I laughed, "Not bad for a floundering poet."

When we reached my block, Kurt stopped in front of Old Man Harvey's house. "Hey, those are the first daffodils I've seen this year."

"Spring flowers put me in a good mood."

"Are you much of a gardener?" he asked.

"No, but my grandmother is. Would you like to meet her? That's my house over there." I couldn't believe my mouth was saying the words. I never dreamed I'd invite Kurt, of all people, home with me. But suddenly I knew it was exactly what I should have done months ago.

"Sure," he replied enthusiastically.

Gram was in the kitchen making dinner. I introduced her to Kurt, and she made a colossal fuss over him. I almost died when she asked him about his parents, but Kurt didn't seem to mind. At last, she gave us a bag of pretzels and two sodas and shooed us outside.

"Sorry about that," I said as we went out on the front porch. "Gram enjoys interrogating my friends."

"I have a grandmother just like her," Kurt's eyes twinkled. The girls had been right about the eyes. They were like sapphires. Why hadn't they impressed me before?

We moved two wicker rockers into a patch of sunlight. "Have you earned your money for the Washington trip yet?" Kurt asked as he passed the pretzels.

"Yes, after plenty of baby-sitting and some yard work. How about you?"

"I have one more job to do Friday. I've washed so many cars in the past three weeks, I could do it in my sleep."

"I can't wait until we go. The trip is probably the best part of being in the honor society."

Kurt put his feet up on the wooden railing and stretched out his legs. "I lived in Washington for a year. It's a fascinating city. The Smithsonian Institution is my favorite place. Have you ever been there?"

"Once, a couple of years ago. I liked the mummies."

"There's no accounting for taste." He wrinkled his nose and we both giggled.

Before I knew it, the bag of pretzels was empty and our patch of sunlight had disappeared. Gram stuck her head out the door. "Your mother and brother will be home any minute, Jennifer. I need the table set."

"I'd better get going," Kurt said, looking at his watch. "I enjoyed talking with you so much, I guess I lost track of time."

"Me too." Why does time go faster when you don't want it to?

"We'll do it again," he said as I walked out to the street with him.

"Can I tell you something, Kurt?" I don't know what made me want to say it, but the words came tumbling out. "I really wanted to beat you today."

"I wanted to win too, Jeffi."

"Does it bother you that we tied?"

He looked at me the way he had that Halloween night in The Alley. Straight into me. Past all the hedges and fences I'd been putting in his way all year long. "I know how you feel about being the best in the class. I like being Number One too. Maybe it's better that we tied this time."

I nodded.

A smile crept onto his face. "But just this once. I don't want to make a habit out of it."

"Neither do I." I laughed. "You'll have to work harder if you want to beat me next time.

"You can count on it!" He reached for my hand. A warm feeling swept over me. "Since we have that settled, I was wondering if you'd like to go to a movie at the mall with me Saturday afternoon."

"I'd love to!"

"Great! We can ride our bikes over. That is, if you don't mind taking bikes. I have a learner's permit but no driver's license yet."

"I don't mind. It would be fun."

He squeezed my hand gently. "See you tomorrow, Jeffi."

I waved as he jogged down the street. What a surprise the afternoon had been! And what a surprise Kurt was! I'd been so busy being jealous of him all year, I never saw what he was really like. Gram was right. You can be wrong about people if you don't look deeply enough.

"This is so romantic!" Sara squealed when I told her the next morning about my afternoon with Kurt. "I knew you two belonged together. Pete thinks so too."

"Don't make this into some sentimental love story. We're only going to the movies."

"Admit it. You like him, and more than just a little."

"OK, he's really nice." I tried my best to sound nonchalant.

"And cute?"

"Yeah, he's cute too."

"Didn't I tell you?" She giggled. "Wait until Mona hears this."

"She'll claim I dragged Kurt to my house and tortured him until he asked me out."

"She had her opportunity, but Kurt knows a good thing when he sees it."

"There you go again."

"It's true! Now tell me what you did when he was at your house."

I shifted my books to the other arm. "We sat on my porch and pigged out on pretzels for two hours."

"What'd you talk about all that time?"

"School, that sort of thing. I don't know. I didn't take notes."

"Ha! I bet you remember every word, every look, every smile."

I didn't want her to know she was right. "You watch too many soap operas."

We approached the school just as a bus pulled up. All the courtyard benches were occupied. "There won't be anybody waiting in the lobby this morning," said Sara. "I hate sitting in classes when spring gets here."

We plopped down on a patch of grass near the steps. "Kurt used to live in Washington," I said. "He promised to show us the best exhibits in the Smithsonian next Saturday."

Sara plucked a yellow dandelion from the lawn and crushed it in her hand. "I'm not sure I'll be going."

"Why not?"

"Money," she said quietly.

"I thought you had all your Rent-a-Kid jobs lined up."

"I did. I would have earned $25 this Saturday washing Mrs. Whitaker's windows and trimming the grass at church."

"So what's the problem? We don't have to turn in the money until Monday."

The 8:45 bell rang. Sara picked up her books and started for the door. I grabbed her arm. "What's going on? Maybe I can help."

"There's nothing you can do." She shrugged. "My parents have to go to a family funeral in Pittsburgh. They'll be gone all weekend and I have to stay with my brothers."

"Maybe your parents would lend you the $25. You could pay them back later. Mrs. Whitaker and the church probably wouldn't mind waiting a couple of weekends."

Sara shook her head. "I can't ask my parents for money. You know things have been tight."

"But you told me your father was doing fix-it jobs around town."

"He doesn't earn much doing those jobs. If there were any way they could help me, they'd have done it already."

I never realized how hard things really were for the Hercheks. Sara had barely mentioned it since Christmas. I assumed that since her parents were both working, everything was all right. "Maybe I could lend you the money. I have some saved."

"No." She frowned. "This isn't your problem. Besides my parents wouldn't let me take charity from anyone. Even you."

"This isn't charity. It's a loan. If you told Mr. Roscher, he could. . ."

"Let's go. I want to put the birthday card I made for Pete in his locker before he gets to school." She glanced over her shoulder at me as we went in the front door. "And stop worrying."

All through homeroom, I couldn't think of anything else. It wasn't fair that Sara had planned for this trip since February and now couldn't go. There had to be some way she could get the money. If only she weren't so stubborn about borrowing it.

By the time Mr. Mowrer took attendance, I had an idea. If I baby-sat with her brothers on Saturday, Sara could do her Rent-a-Kid jobs. There was only one problem — what to do about my date with Kurt. I couldn't think of any other way. If I were going to help Sara, I'd have to break my date with Kurt.

What if he didn't understand? After the way I had treated him all year, he might think I was giving him the brush-off. But I couldn't tell him the real reason because that would embarrass Sara. I was taking a big risk. He might never ask me out again.

I pulled Sara into the girls' room on the way to first period and explained my plan. At first, she wouldn't listen. "I told you I didn't want to discuss this. I'll get to Washington another time."

"This is the perfect solution. There's no reason why you can't do it."

She stared at the floor. "My parents won't be able to pay you."

"I know and it's all right. I like your little brothers."

"What about your date with Kurt?"

"We didn't decide which day we'd go. I'll suggest Sunday." A white lie was allowed just this once.

"Sure you don't mind?"

I shook my head. Sara threw her arms around my neck. "Thanks, Jeffi! I won't forget this."

I hoped Kurt had the same reaction.

Kurt waited for me after every class that day. It was fun walking down the halls with him, laughing over something a teacher had said, or commiserating about how much homework we had. I didn't want to spoil it by breaking our date although I knew there was no use putting it off.

Yet I couldn't find the right moment. I almost told him on the way from history to math. Then I noticed Mona and LuAnn, with their radar ears, walking behind us. On the way out of math, Kurt and Pete kidded around about Mr. Trimble's new sport coat, and I couldn't get a word in. Last period, I had a study hall and Kurt had P.E. When the three-o'clock bell rang, I still hadn't done it.

While I took my books and sweater from the locker, I watched for Kurt to return from the gym. As kids rushed for their buses, the crowd cleared. By 3:15, the hall was nearly deserted and I was late for band practice. If Kurt didn't show up soon, I'd have to call him tonight. What if he hung up on me?

At last, I spotted him, coming around the corner with a towel rolled up under his arm. He waved when he saw me. "Can you wait while I get my books?" he called.

"Sure." I nervously tapped my fingers on the locker. What should I say? I could tell him my mother wouldn't let me go. Or I had to fill in at Ralph's office because Paula was sick. Or my bike had a flat. No. I didn't want to lie to him. I couldn't think of a convincing one anyway.

"The coach had a broken watch," Kurt said, dropping his books on the floor next to me. He tucked in the tail of his knit shirt. "I raced out of the showers. I was afraid you'd be gone." He smiled engagingly.

I must be crazy to do this. "Kurt, there's something I have to tell you. I hope you'll understand." I stared at my notebook cover where I'd drawn a heart around our names. "I can't go to the movies with you Saturday."

"Why not?" he asked.

"I can't tell you. I wish I could, but it's kind of personal."

"I hope things are OK with your family."

"It's nothing like that. It's just that a complication developed that I didn't know about yesterday."

"Oh." His smile was completely gone now. "I'm sorry you can't go."

"I am too. I really am."

Kurt picked up his books. "Mind if I walk you home? I want to show you something I saw this morning."

"I can't. I have practice for my solo in the Spring Concert." For the first time, I wished I didn't have that solo I'd worked so hard for.

"I can wait for you."

"I won't be finished until five. My mom's picking me up on her way home from work."

Kurt's eyes shifted away from me. His jaw muscles twitched the way Ralph's do when he gets upset. It's not what you're thinking, Kurt!

"Maybe we can go to the movies another time." Please, please ask me for Sunday.

"Yeah, maybe we can," he replied flatly. "Well, I don't want to make you late. See you later." He turned on his heel and stalked away.

Why did this have to happen just when our relationship had started to soar? Was this a crash landing?

12

I had a glimmer of hope that the situation wasn't as gloomy as it seemed. Tomorrow Kurt would wait for me after every class and we'd eat lunch together. He'd apologize for jumping to conclusions and then invite me to the movies on Sunday.

That glimmer faded by first period. I was in biology lab doing a frog dissection. I reached the section where I had to examine the frog's leg muscles, and all the microscopes were in use. Mrs. Amadon sent me to the storage room to get another. When I opened the door, there was Kurt with his head in a cabinet.

"Hi," I said, in my most cheerful voice.

He pulled a microscope off the shelf, then closed the cabinet door. "Don't forget to turn off the light when you leave."

"I need a microscope too." I took a few steps toward him.

"There's one left." He brushed past me and walked out the door. No friendly smile. No meaningful look. Nothing but the coldest shoulder this side of the Arctic Circle. It became more frigid as the week progressed. I couldn't help feeling that as far as Kurt was concerned, Jeffi Anders had ceased to exist.

The worst moment was at the honor society meeting the following Tuesday. Kurt arrived late and most of the seats were taken. He could have sat in the empty chair next to me or in the corner with some other sophomore guys. Instead he unfolded a chair that rested against the wall and placed it next to Mona.

While Mr. Roscher discussed last-minute details of our Washington trip, the two of them had their heads together whispering and laughing. Mona touched Kurt's arm so many times she probably developed calluses on her fingers and he looked as if he were enjoying it. Watching them made my blood boil. If only I could explain everything to him.

Even though Kurt and I had had the shortest romance in the history of Daniel Boone High, I still felt miserable about its ending. It would have helped if there were someone to talk to about it. I couldn't let Sara know what was happening because she'd figure out the truth about my helping her. As for Bethany, who had a solution to every problem, she had kept her distance since that episode over Mike.

That's why I almost dropped my tray in shock when Bethany butted in the lunch line between Sara and me on Thursday. "Mind if I sit with you?" she asked sheepishly.

"Where's Lover Boy today?" said Sara.

"I'm so mad I could . . . Oh, I don't know what!" she snarled. "If I never see Frank's face again, it would be too soon!"

Sara and I exchanged puzzled glances as the three of us sat down at a table near the back of the cafeteria.

"What in the world happended?" I asked.

Bethany gritted her teeth. She looked ready to explode any second. "That jerk didn't call me last night as he usually does. I wasted the entire evening waiting too. Even passed up a chance to go shopping at the new store in the mall with my mother and aunt just so I wouldn't miss his call. When Kevin came home, he said he saw Frank at The Alley."

"That's no reason to get so angry," I said.

"With another girl!"

"Uh-oh," I moaned.

Bethany's eyes began to water. She blinked hard to clear them, but it was no use. "This morning . . ." Her voice cracked. ". . . this morning I confronted Frank about it. He claimed she was his cousin from Massachusetts and his parents were making him entertain her."

"Maybe she *is* his cousin," Sara said reassuringly.

Bethany shook her head. "Kevin's date knew her from St. Pius. She's a cheerleader there."

Sara put her arm around Bethany's shoulder. "Maybe you and Frank can work this out."

"Never!" she hissed. "Not after what that long-legged spider did when I told him I knew the truth." She pulled a tissue from her purse and dabbed her eyes. "Right in the middle of the lobby, in front of everyone, he laughed at me! Then he said he'd been seeing her for for three weeks. And if I didn't like it, too bad. Three weeks!"

"Try not to cry, Beth," I said. "You're smearing your make-up."

Bethany sniffed and wiped her cheeks. "You're right. I don't want to give Frank the satisfaction of seeing me cry over him."

After school, the three of us went to my house and made sundaes. While Sara and I concocted the butterscotch-whipped cream-chocolate chips-vanilla ice cream-maraschino cherry masterpieces, Bethany sat at the kitchen table complaining about Frank between mouthfuls of chocolate chips. "What am I going to do about the prom?"

"Good grief, Beth! That's six weeks away!" exclaimed Sara.

"It's not too early to think about it. At least Frank didn't do this to me later. Then I'd never find a date in time."

"You sure recovered fast." I plopped a cherry into my mouth.

"There are plenty of other fish in the sea, right?"

"And it won't take you long to hook a new one," giggled Sara.

Bethany got up from the table and went to the window. "Next time, I'm going to be more choosy about what I reel in," she murmured as she rested her elbows on the sill. "I was pretty rotten to you two. Thanks for taking me back even though I behaved like a real moron the past couple of weeks."

"Forget it," said Sara.

Bethany looked at me. "I'm sorry I gave you a hard time. You were right about guys like Mike Hauser. Forgive me?"

"Of course. I'm just glad everything's straightened out. Now dig in before your ice cream turns to soup." I handed her a spoon. "It feels great to be friends again."

If only I could say those words to Kurt too.

I almost expected to wake up the next morning miraculously transformed into a glowing, sophisticated woman. Instead I felt and looked like that some old Jeffi. What a disappointment!

"Happy birthday!" Mom, Gram, and Ralph sang when I walked into the kitchen for breakfast. On the table sat three brightly wrapped packages.

"Hurry and open them," said Ralph. "I'm dying of curiosity."

I picked up the large, flat box first. It was from Gram. "Pretty paper," I said as I carefully slipped my fingernail under the tape.

"Oh, go on and rip it," she replied. "It isn't every day you turn sweet 16."

I pushed aside the tissue paper. Inside was a luscious ocean-blue, floor-length skirt and a white-lace blouse with ruffled collar.

"It's for your Spring Concert." Gram smiled. "I thought it was time you had a new dressy outfit. I picked it out myself."

"But, Gram, you hate shopping."

"This was special, dear."

"Thank you. I love it." Next was a small, square package from Ralph. I lifted the lid to find a piece of paper. "It's an I.O.U. for driving lessons! You're willing to teach me to drive?" I asked him incredulously.

"I think I can handle the assignment," he replied, laughing.

"Thank you from *me*, Ralph," interjected Mom.

I couldn't believe my eyes when I opened the last package. "A make-up kit! It has everything."

"The woman at Howland's said all the colors would match your complexion. I showed her your photograph to be sure."

"It's terrific, Mom!" I hugged her.

"I decided if you could run this household for six weeks, you were old enough to wear make-up. I guess I didn't realize how grown-up you've become."

Ralph winked at me.

"Thank you, everybody!" Suddenly, 16 *did* seem special. And I felt like a brand-new Jeffi!

After school, Sara and Bethany took me to The Alley. "A toast!" Bethany said as we clinked glasses and gulped down our sodas.

"Let's dig in," said Sara.

"Don't drool. It's unbecoming," teased Bethany as she sliced The Alley's complimentary cake. "This looks delicious. You can bring me here on my birthday."

"You'll have to put up with the entire place singing to you first," I reminded her. My face was still red from when three waiters had carried the cake to our table while 30 people stared.

"How's it feel to be 16?" Sara asked.

"Not bad," I replied, grinning.

"Just think," said Bethany dramatically, "you're almost a woman."

"I wouldn't go *that* far," I grumbled. "Here I am—sweet 16 and never been kissed. Even my first date was a total disaster."

"Don't give up yet," said Bethany.

"Sure," Sara added. "Good things have a way of happening when you least expect it."

Mr. Roscher told us to be at the school by 6:00 A.M. Saturday "or the bus will go without you." I couldn't imagine his actually leaving the parking lot while some kid frantically ran down Washington Street in pursuit. But to be safe, I set the alarm for 4:45.

The sky had a faint pink tint when Ralph dropped me off. Despite the fact that he still wore his pajamas under his jacket and his eyes were half-open, he didn't once complain about getting up at 5:30. In fact, when he heard I planned to walk to school that morning, he insisted on driving. "It's too dark at that hour. Besides I have to go to the office early." In spite of what he said, I knew

Ralph would crawl right back into bed as soon as he got home.

As I hopped out of the car, I spotted Sara and Cheryl next to the Greyhound. "You didn't want to miss the bus either."

"Are you kidding?" laughed Cheryl. "Not after the work I did to go on this trip."

"It's too early." Sara yawned. "I think Mr. Roscher just wanted to see us suffer."

"The early bird gets the worm," said a voice behind us. There was Mona twirling a curl around her index finger. She wore a new pair of culottes, a tailored jacket, and soft leather boots. She made me feel like a mannequin from the Goodwill store.

"Looks like you spent half the night getting ready, Mona," said Sara. "This is only a field trip, not a fashion show."

" 'Be prepared' is my motto." She adjusted her shoulder bag and strolled away.

"I wonder which guy she's after this time," Cheryl said in a low voice.

"I know," Sara replied glancing at me, "but she's wasting her time."

"I'm not so sure." The image of the honor society meeting flashed across my mind. "Sara, let's be sure to sit at the other end of the bus from her."

"Cheryl and I are sitting together," Sara said matter-of-factly.

I couldn't believe my ears. After everything that had happened, was Sara dumping me to sit with Cheryl? And without telling me? "But I assumed you and I would be partners."

"You shouldn't have. Sorry."

"What am I supposed to do now? I'll have to sit alone for four hours. Or worse yet, next to somebody no one else wants for a partner."

"I'm sure something will work out." Sara shrugged casually.

Tears welled in my eyes. How could she do this to me? I rushed to an empty bench near the far end of the courtyard. I wanted to run home and hide under my covers.

A few minutes later, Kurt drove up with his father. If people wondered why Mona was dressed to kill this morning, they found out the moment Kurt got out of the car. Using her most seductive moves, Mona slithered over to him.

Now I regretted going on this trip. How could I enjoy a single minute of it when my best friend didn't want to be with me and Mona had her claws into Kurt?

I couldn't bear to watch how he returned her greeting. Turning my attention from the disgusting scene, I faced the playing fields. A flock of robins pecked at the wet ground. Mona wasn't the only early bird to get her worm this morning.

I didn't realize someone had approached the bench until I felt a touch on my arm. Was I surprised!

"Why are you being so antisocial?" Kurt sat down next to me.

"I felt like doing a little bird-watching."

"Oh, I see," he replied, looking toward the field. He shifted his eyes back to me. "Are you sitting with anyone in particular on the bus?"

"I thought so, but Sara made other plans," I said, feeling both embarassed and angry.

"How about sitting with me?" He raised his eyebrows expectantly.

I didn't get it. His words didn't fit the way he'd been acting all week. "I thought you and Mona . . ."

"What about her?"

"Nothing. I thought you were . . . well . . . you certainly seemed angry with me for breaking our date last weekend."

"Sara explained the whole situation as soon as she found out about it. Pete had mentioned how upset I was, and she put two and two together."

"I'm sorry I couldn't tell you the truth."

"I understand. It was a nice thing you did for Sara." He put his hand on top of mine and squeezed gently. "What about seeing the movie next Saturday afternoon?"

"Uh-oh."

"What is it this time?" He rolled his eyes.

"The Spring Concert is that night. I have to be home by 4:00 to get ready. We'd never get back in time."

"You don't make it easy for a guy, do you?" He laughed. "How about this? Instead of the movie, we'll go on a bike hike in the morning, have a picnic lunch, and you can get home by 4:00."

"That sounds perfect!"

Kurt let out an exaggerated sigh. "Finally! Now that we've settled that, let's get going before Roscher leaves us behind. Do you like the window or aisle seat?"

"Why don't we trade halfway?" I said, as we ran toward the bus.

"Good idea!" Kurt caught my hand as we crossed the courtyard together.

In a few short moments, I had gone from the pits to a pinnacle, and I was still rising.

The rest of the day was better than my most blissful dream, even better than my most exciting fantasy. Kurt and I spent the entire bus ride talking and laughing together. It didn't even bother me when Mona, sitting two seats in front of us, kept turning to look at Kurt. I knew I didn't have to worry about her any more.

The day passed quickly. Being with Kurt was easy and natural. Unlike my dates with Mike, I didn't have to pretend to be someone else. It was the *real* Jeffi Kurt liked.

We raced up the Washington Monument—he won by 35 steps. Later we were separated from the group in the Smithsonian and almost missed the bus to the White House. The most interesting stop was the Capitol. I learned more from Kurt than from the tour guide.

"How did you find out so much about Congress?" I asked him as we sat in the visitors' gallery.

"It's only because my dad worked in government. You hear all the behind-the-scenes stories that way."

"Wouldn't it be wonderful to stand there and debate an important bill?" I pointed to the podium below. "Just think, you could influence the course of history."

Kurt smiled. "I can see you doing that in 20 years. Congresswoman Jennifer Anders."

"Senator," I corrected him.

By the time we climbed onto the bus for the last time, I was exhausted. My feet felt like heavy rocks dangling at the ends of my legs. And I wasn't the only one. As we drove toward home, the excited buzz of voices quieted to a mere murmur, heads nodded, and seat backs lowered.

"My shoulder isn't occupied," whispered Kurt. "It's not as soft as a pillow, but you're welcome to use it."

I rested my cheek against his shoulder and closed my eyes. I fell asleep listening to the steady rhythm of his breathing. It was the sweetest lullaby I'd ever heard.

The weather report called for rain, but I knew the forecast was wrong. It wouldn't dare rain. Not this day. The sky was crystal clear except for an occasional puffy, white cloud drifting by. Beads of sparkling dew covered the lawn, which was just starting to show its deep, summer green.

"Spring's here at last!" Kurt shouted as we pedaled toward the outskirts of town.

"After the winter we had, I'm glad to see the trees budding. I don't even mind bugs buzzing around again."

"We're almost there," Kurt said turning onto Mingo Creek Road. "First we ride along the creek for about a mile."

"I've never been out here on a bike before. It's so peaceful."

"I hope you like the spot I chose for our picnic. It's right up ahead."

The narrow road crossed an old stone bridge, then curved away from the creek toward open farmland. We leaned our bikes against a large oak tree at the edge of the field. Weaving our way through rows of dried cornstalk stumps left over from the fall harvest, we headed across the field.

At the far end, Kurt stopped. "That's the place." He pointed to a stream trickling below us. "The bank looks steep, but it's not hard to climb down. There are plenty of rocks to use as footholds. I'll go first and show you the way."

Following him, I eased down—mostly on the seat of my jeans. When I finally reached the stream, I knew the descent had been worth the effort. Tall trees along the bank formed a curtain around us. The soothing sounds of chirping birds and water bubbling over rocks filled the valley. Kurt had found a secret sanctuary.

"I've lived here all my life, but I never knew about this." I dipped my fingers into the cool water.

"It's a special place. I wanted to share it with you." Our eyes met. For a long, marvelous moment, I was hypnotized by his gaze.

"Let's sit on the big rock over there in the sun." He spoke softly, as if he were afraid to break the spell.

"Look, wild flowers. Do you know what they are?"

Shaking his head, he stooped to pick one, then handed it to me. I fastened it under my barrette. He smiled admiringly.

Kurt crawled onto the rock and reached down to pull me up. His grasp was strong. Removing our knapsacks, we stretched out on the smooth granite.

"Are you ready for your concert tonight?" he asked.

"I hope so."

"I'm coming, you know."

"You are?"

"Sure. I don't want to miss your solo. Pete says you're pretty good."

"I'm OK, I guess."

"You must be better than OK if you have a solo."

I remembered the challenge with Norma. "There's another girl who's just as good. I'll have to stay on my toes when we try out for junior-senior band next year."

"I heard you had a birthday last week," Kurt said, reaching into his knapsack.

"How did you know?"

"I have my sources." He pulled out a small object neatly wrapped in tissue paper and placed it in my hand.

I unfolded the paper. Inside was a ceramic pendant attached to a gold chain. Delicately painted on the front was a purple crocus. "It's gorgeous, Kurt. Did you make it?"

He nodded. "One morning a few weeks ago, I saw a crocus like that one poking through the snow—a flower strong enough to break through the frozen ground, yet beautiful and glowing." He leaned toward me and gently touched my cheek with his warm fingers. "It reminded me of you, Jeffi."

"You made this just for me?"

"I always thought you were different from other girls. But for so long I couldn't get you to look at me twice." He smiled. "I'm glad I finally have the chance to show you how I feel."

"I'm glad I finally realized how I felt about you."

The next thing I knew, Kurt's lips were on mine. A tingly sensation rushed through me. My first kiss! Not like spin the bottle when it didn't mean anything, but a *real* kiss. Something special and wonderful. From a *very* Special Someone!

"I know it's more than a month away," Kurt said as he tenderly held my hand, "but would you be my date for the prom? I'll have my license by then."

"I'd like to go with you even if we had to take our bikes."

Kurt laughed. "Wearing a formal?"

"Even then. There isn't anyone I'd rather be with than you." I meant it from deep in my heart.

Playing games didn't bring me love and happiness. And flirting and pretending didn't help me find my Special Someone. All it took was being myself.